The Penket
Papers

The Penket Papers

AND OTHER STORIES

Colin Richmond

ALAN SUTTON
1986

Alan Sutton Publishing Limited
30 Brunswick Road   Gloucester

First published 1986

British Library Cataloguing in Publication Data

Richmond, Colin
The Penket papers.
I. Title
823'.914 [F]   PR6068.I2/

ISBN 0-86299-278-8

Typesetting and origination by
Alan Sutton Publishing Limited
Photoset Century Schoolbook 11/13
Printed in Great Britain

for
Hugh Leech

Preface

I have called these pieces *Merzgeschichte* in homage to their original inspirer: Kurt Schwitters. Beyond that there is no need to go; as Proust said, 'A work of art which contains theories is like an article on which the price-ticket has been left'. For their encouragement I would like to thank Margaret Buxton, Geoffrey O'Connor, Barrie Dobson, Dom Daniel Rees, Stefan Themerson, and above all Myrna Richmond.

'Kurt Schwitters in England' was published in *Zweitschrift* 4/5 (Hannover, Spring 1979) and, under the title 'Eine seltsame Begegnung', in the *Kurt Schwitters Almanach* for 1982. 'The day Henry James discovered Dada' appeared in *Encounter* 313 for October 1979. 'A Blatter of Rain and the Origins of Penkhull' was published in *The Downside Review* of April 1983, 'St Penket's Leg and Boot' in the same journal, July 1984. 'A Blatter of Rain' has also appeared in Jorge Luis Borges, *Le Martin Fierro* (Paris, 1985), under the title 'A Blatter of Rain et les origines de Penkhull'.

Contents

1

A Blatter of Rain
and the Origins of Penkhull

FRIBOURG in Switzerland is for me a memorable place as it was the scene of my first mystical experience – but that is another story for another occasion. What else had happened to me there on 13th August 1954 submerged without trace until I read this passage of Proust about two years ago. Then, in perfect Proustian fashion it returned. This is the passage:

> Now the memories of love are no exception to the general laws of memory, which in turn are governed by the still more general laws of Habit. And as Habit weakens everything, what best reminds us of a person is precisely what we had forgotten (because it was of no importance, and we therefore left it in full possession of its strength). That is why the better part of our memories exists outside us, in a blatter of rain, in the smell of an unaired room or of the first crackling brushwood fire in a cold grate: wherever, in short, we happen upon what our mind, having no use for it, has rejected, the last treasure that the past has in store, the richest, that which, when all our flow of tears seems to have dried at the source, can make us weep again. Outside us? Within us, rather, but hidden from our eyes in an

1

oblivion more or less prolonged. It is thanks to this oblivion alone that we can from time to time recover the person that we were, place ourselves in relation to things as he was placed, suffer anew because we are no longer ourselves but he, and because he loved what now leaves us indifferent. In the broad daylight of our habitual memory the images of the past turn gradually pale and fade out of sight, nothing remains of them, we shall never recapture it. Or rather we should never recapture it had not a few words . . . been carefully locked away in oblivion, just as an author deposits in the National Library a copy of a book which might otherwise become unobtainable.

It was the phrase 'a blatter of rain' which was for me the equivalent of Proust's madeleine in lemon tea or his uneven curb-stone. On reading it, all at once I was pushing my bicycle across the cobbles of the Rue des Epousses in a sudden spurt of rain which came out of a hot blue sky; children ran shouting into doorways, up alleys. Before me the tower of the cathedral rose blocking my way; then, to my left, a narrow entrance between two houses appeared, I turned down it, parked my bike against a wall, went through a door and was in a hall shaking the rain off me and paying admission to the cathedral museum to an elderly attendant.

The museum was a jumble of objects: rare and precious alongside the commonplace and banal. I was ready to escape as the sun came flooding into a particularly dingy room containing a cabinet of reliquaries, mainly modern gilt and glass affairs. My middle-class Protestant stomach began to turn, yet I had recently seen the head of St Oswald at Zug and my recollection of that remarkable sight, which had impressed me despite myself, made me look along the rows of reliquaries. Parts of St Jost, St Nicholas, and St Leonard, one of the thirty pieces of silver, a napkin from the last supper, some of the needles by which St Beatus had suffered martyrdom, and nailparings of the Blessed Virgin. There was nothing to delay me here. But at the end, pushed back slightly, there was a large, square and empty box of crystal. The label propped against it – and here I have consulted, as you will realize I have also for the objects just listed, my notebooks of that Swiss summer – the label read: 'this held the head of St Penket, stolen in 1868'

Can such a Proustian recovery of the past ever have had such strange and scholarly consequences as those which I am about to narrate?

Soon after my remembrance of things past and return to my 'juvenilia' of the mid-fifties I was looking through D. W. Rollason's recent edition of the tenth-century *List of Saints' Resting Places in Anglo-Saxon England*. There featured the body of St Penket, claimed by Much Wenlock. A footnote informed me that St Penket was otherwise unknown, save for a twelfth-century Leominster Abbey relic list, published in the *Proceedings of the Woolhope Club* for October 1868 by the great liturgical scholar Edmund Bishop, which claimed a head of St Penket. When I finally found this obscure paper Bishop's comment on Leominster's claim was striking:

St Penket's body was at Wenlock, according to the tenth-century list of saints' resting places, and it was probably still there in the twelfth century. Leominster's claim to possess the head in the 1150s, however, is patently false; though it had indeed been stolen from Much Wenlock in one of the earliest recorded, perhaps *the* earliest theft of relics, it was by Irish monks who eventually settled at Pfaffengarten near Fribourg in Switzerland around the year 700. Their community faded away in the eleventh century, which was probably when St Penket's head found its way into the cathedral of St Nicholas at Fribourg where it was until recently. Nothing is known of St Penket save that her feast day was, according to the single surviving calendar of the Pfaffengarten house, 10th December, and that she can only have been, because of her name and the identity of her robbers, an Irish, that is a Celtic saint, a putative companion of St Chad or St Bertolin or even St Mildburga.

What fascinated me at this point was not St Penket (with whom I as yet had no thought of connecting Penkhull), but the conjunction of those dates: the theft of the head and Bishop's knowledge of it in an article of the same year. Had the theft been splashed all over *The Times*? Perhaps at least it had been mentioned, and anyway Bishop was likely to have had other ways of knowing such things; still I was sufficiently intrigued and in the next Easter vacation not too busy to pursue Edmund Bishop into his journals and working papers at Downside Abbey.

I was rewarded. He had been in Switzerland in 1868, a little, but not much, older than I had been in 1954, but far more sympathetic to saints – he had converted to Catholicism in 1867 – and already learned in a way I shall never be. His notebooks of his journey down the Rhine to Switzerland and Italy in 1868 disclose the man who would write so sensitively about European saints, who is revered as the founding father of the systematic study of the development of the Roman and local Western liturgies, and whose knowledge of the monastic and other ecclesiastical sources of the mediaeval West was so wide-ranging and deep that among his many triumphs was the identification of a bone of St Thomas Cantilupe at Hereford. Yet so retiring a man was he that little of his labours was published under his own name: he preferred to allow others to use his work and did not overly mind to see it appear in print with the barest acknowledgment to himself. So, through Nigel Abercrombie's biography of him, had I come to know him. So, to some extent, he was already revealed in the 1868 journal. But as I pored over it in the solitude of the library at Downside it became clear that there had been more to him in 1868 than Mr Abercrombie had let on. As a biographer Mr Abercrombie had not come clean.

Not on one matter anyway. Edmund Bishop, who later tried his monastic vocation at Downside and, though that way was not for him, remained a lifelong bachelor, had had in the summer of 1868 a female companion between Basle and Geneva. He referred to her only as FH. She was lively, liked dancing – at Neuchâtel he recorded their presence at a ball until after midnight, at Berne they danced in the street during the festival – and he evidently had respect for her intelligence as three times he set down her opinions of churches. He is reticent and she hardly comes alive for us, but I believe I detected more than mere affection in those sparse entries. At Geneva she disappears from his pages. He does not mention her going nor does he ever refer to her again.

There was more. In the itinerary Fribourg does not feature. They went from Berne to Lausanne, then by Nyon to Geneva. There is no mention of Fribourg through which they would certainly have passed, indeed did pass, for they were at Berne on 9th July and Edmund's next entry is for 11th July at Lausanne: they cannot have gone by any other route in so short a time. Thus, with the light going from the library windows I was sitting stock still staring at Edmund's densely written pages without seeing them. I had put two and two together – as you have done – and arrived at the barely credible question:

5

could Edmund Bishop have stolen St Penket's head on 10th July 1868?

Before I left Downside I made another small discovery which did nothing to lessen my feeling that at the very least Edmund had something to hide. I checked the drafts of his *Dublin Review* paper of 1887, 'Notes on Some Relics of English Saints Abroad', which in its published form has no mention of St Penket. In his first draft, however, he does mention her head at Fribourg and its theft 'sometime in the 1860's'. In subsequent revisions that brief notice has been taken out. The mature Edmund (he was 40 in 1887) was more circumspect than the precocious 24-year-old scholar of 1868. To me it seemed certain: he did have something to hide.

You can imagine with what alacrity I wrote to the Dean and Chapter at Fribourg, and with what keyed-up anticipation I awaited their reply. Would it say 10th July 1868? It did, of course, or you would not be reading this now. The Dean wrote, 'Who would have done such a thing? It has remained a mystery from that day to this. Let us know if you discover anything.'

Clearly, what I had now to try to discover was where St Penket's head had gone and whether the mysterious FH had anything to do with its disappearance. There remained as a potential and accessible source Bishop's letters, some at the British Library but most in private hands. Nevertheless, it was his correspondence of the years around 1870 which mattered most and here, though I drew a blank at the British Library, I was immediately fortunate thereafter. His letters of this time to Baron Friedrich von Hügel are in the University Library of St Andrews, so I turned next to them. They disclosed what I was hoping to find: who FH was. In the one letter to von Hügel of the summer of

1868, dated from Berne on 7th July, Edmund writes of her enthusiastically as 'a vivacious young woman travelling with a family party, 23 like me and great good company, intelligent, full of fun but serious too you know, not in the least pious let alone mystical, my dear Hügel, so not a woman for you – but certainly for me in my holiday mood'. He then went on to describe their enjoyment of the festival at Berne, boating on the river, a visit to the parliament house, the theatre, and so on. She was called Fanny Haslam.

There was one other unexpected and startling piece of information he supplied: she came from the Potteries. Thus, once again I was to sit transfixed in another library, staring out over the grey sea across the bay to Leucars air base, from which aeroplanes rose to defend me from Russian nuclear attack. I sat unmoved for a long time because I knew who Fanny Haslam was. As the *Evening Sentinel* once put it, 'Fanny Haslam was a remarkable woman. She died at the age of 90 in 1935 and her remembrance of her homeland and interest in its culture never waned. . . .' She had died in Argentina and I knew of her because her grandson is one of the world's most magical writers and one of my favourties, Jorge Luis Borges. He had come to the Potteries in 1963, the year before I did, to visit his grandmother's birth-place.

If I was sitting unmoved, my mind was racing. I cannot remember leaving the library and walking along North Street and down to the harbour, but that is where, so to speak, I came to. What had I arrived at? An impressionable Edmund Bishop, Jorge Luis Borges' adventurous and beautiful grandmother, and their theft, their possible, their very probable theft of an expatriate British saint's head from a Swiss cathedral. It seemed too far-

fetched to be true, but that is where the facts had
inexorably led me. More than that; the evidence was
revealing other avenues of enquiry up which my
racing mind was speeding that warm, breezeless
evening in St Andrews. There was, for instance,
Fanny's love of her homeland – and we of the
Potteries know what that means of a born and bred
Potter – and her enthusiasm for its culture; there
was Edmund Bishop's knowledge of the English
religious past, in 1868 already considerable and
likely to include St Penket and her first theft; there
was Jorge Luis Borges' story of 1963, 'The Villas of
Don Julio Cortazar', set in an unrecognizable but
unmistakably named Penkhull, just as his earlier
and more famous story, 'The Garden of Forking
Paths', had been set in an unrecognizable Fenton;
and finally there was the writer's pilgrimage to
Fanny's home in that same year.

I have not, so far, pursued the Argentinian end of
the story, though I do know that Fanny went to join
her married sister in Argentina in the autumn of
1868, and that in 1870 in the provincial capital of
Parana at a ball – where else – she met and fell in
love with Colonel Francisco Borges whom she soon
afterwards married. It was her lawyer son of Buenos
Aires who was Jorge Luis' father. I have tried
harder where St Penket is concerned but have not
been able to get any further. I have not found, as
Edmund Bishop did not find (unless he destroyed
anything else he did discover), more about her.
There, I suspect, we are at a literary-documentary
dead end.

Where there has been more to discover, and it is
not only exciting but crucial, has been about Borges'
visit to the Potteries in 1963. That he went to
Fanny's birthplace, 11 Boothroyd Street, Hanley,
was unexciting news, but that he also went to 21

The Villas, on the slope of the hill leading up to Penkhull, was the very opposite. The house turned out to be where Fanny's family had lived in the later 1860s. The *Sentinel* does no more than report his going there and comment on the length of time he spent inside the house with the then owner, Mr Arthur Collis, who is stated to have said in answer to the question, what did the great man do, that the almost completely blind Borges spent a long time going through each room, stopping and peering, that then he had a cup of tea and talked about what a grand lady his grandmother was and how close he and she had been.

Mr Collis, however, was not speaking the truth, or rather he did not tell all that Borges did that afternoon. I traced Mr Collis, who died in March this year, to his son's home at Butterton. I pressed him on the point: what did the great writer do for the three hours he was at 21 The Villas? 'He went into the garden', said Mr Collis, 'and he and that young man who was with him' – that was Borges' constant companion, the American Norman Thomas di Giovanni – 'they buried a box, small it was like this', and he shaped in the air with his hands a box about a foot by a foot square. 'He asked me not to say anything, said it was something of his grandmother's. I don't expect it was anything valuable, do you?'

There I was once more, sitting rigid and staring out into space beyond the garden where St Thomas's neo-Norman church tower was visible through the bare trees. I knew (as you now know) what was in that box. I asked Mr Collis if it was still buried in the garden when he had left the house. That uncurious and, to judge by his son's house, wealthy man told me that so far as he knew it had been.

Let me draw matters to a conclusion. I am as sure

as an historian ever can be that St Penket's head, once at Fribourg, is now buried in the garden of 21 The Villas, Stoke-on-Trent. I am sure Fanny entrusted it to her beloved grandson; perhaps he undertook to bring it when he could to what she regarded as its rightful resting place. That he dutifully and in due course did. But why was Penkhull its home? That we will never know for certain. I think, however, that Edmund told her, somewhere between Basle and Fribourg or perhaps even as they gazed together at the relic itself in the cathedral treasury, of his belief that St Penket came from Penkhull. For I suspect that he believed, as I believe, that she gave her name to the place, that the editor of *The Oxford Dictionary of English Place Names* (through not knowing of her) opted for the apparently more likely explanation – that is, that the name derives from the British 'Penketh', meaning 'end of a wood', and that there was a British place on the hill called that: Penketh – I think there was a British place on the hill alright, but named after the saint who lived and died at the foot of the hill where the marshy land began, where in fact her fellow Celtic saints liked to live, in fenny, watery places – Chad at Lichfield, Guthlac at Crowland, Bertolin at Stafford – where indeed The Villas now are. And I believe Edmund Bishop thought that, and when he learnt where Fanny lived told her too. I rather think it was she who opened the reliquary and carried away St Penket's head, impetuously perhaps, out of local patriotism possibly, out of sheer high spirits and bravado and, I suspect, to impress, even to scandalize the stuffy and proper Edmund. I would guess that it was too much for him, that they fought and parted. That, however, is pure conjecture.

2

St Penket's Leg and Boot

I know that history runs in phases, and we are living in
a phase that forces us to acquire technical knowledge.
But one must always be aware of the great danger that
lies in exclusive specialization. . . . It is equally important to develop sensibility, and the best means to that
end is art – the way it describes, pictures, and gives
testimony to life. – Eva Forest in Christa Wolf, *A Model
Childhood* (English translation, 1983), p. 340.

Among them was a description, shattering in its
literary power, of the theft of some meat-balls from
someone's jacket pocket. . . . – Mikhail Bulgakov, *The
Master and Margarita* (English translation, 1969), p.
104.

WHEN I take those of my students who are studying
'Religion and Art in the later Middle Ages' to
Birmingham it is to see two reliquaries: the first is
modern, is in St Edward's chapel in Pugin's Lubeck-
like Roman Catholic cathedral, and contains St
Chad's thighbone; the second is in the Barber Insti-
tute of Fine Arts at the University, is a mediaeval
German arm reliquary from the Rhineland, and
contains the legbone of St Penket. This is the Barber
Institute's description of their reliquary:

11

It was made, probably in the thirteenth century, to enshrine a piece of bone from the arm of a saint, which was to be displayed beneath a piece of glass inserted at the front. This window-opening was probably made later in the Middle Ages, although the glass is modern. The relic is in fact, however, a fragment of a legbone: such discrepancies are not uncommon in this class of object. The reliquary was brought in 1961 from the dealer Barling. When it was examined and opened in 1962 a strip of parchment, bearing the name of the saint, was found near the relic. Only the letters 'et' of the inscription were legible, and the parchment was so decayed that it decomposed almost instantly when it was exposed to the air.

As we have stood gazing at what appropriately remains of this seventh-century saint, to my knowledge the only whirling or dancing saint in Western Christendom, whose legs were, so to speak, her salvation, I have never told my students that I have seen the reliquary before elsewhere, a long way from the Barber Institute. For a simple reason: I could not remember where. It was not until last summer, to be precise 29th August, the very day *The Times* brought St Penket's head to the notice of the nation, that I was put on the trail of St Penket's leg, a trail which has brought me here to tell you where I once spent a night with the Barber Institute's reliquary and the illustrious relic it enshrined.

On 29th August 1983 I was at Boot in Eskdale, not for the first time; but never previously had I ventured into St Catherine's church which stands beside that beautiful, stoney river. The church, 'a typical dale chapel' (as Pevsner calls it), did not keep me long; on coming out, however, I was attracted by two modern tombstones standing upright and side by side against the churchyard wall; their finely-cut lettering revealed to my astonishment that beneath them lay the bodies of those distinguished historians, Sir Maurice Powicke and his son-in-law, Richard Pares. I had not realized that the Powicke family had anticipated my affection for this valley, that Sir Maurice and Lady Powicke (as *The Times* obituary of 21st May 1963 put it) 'at their cottage in Eskdale seemed a kindly and essential part of Lakeland'. This unexpected encounter impelled me, on returning from holiday, to look at some of the early work of this diminutive historian – tiny in stature and mighty of mind as many must have said of him. There were some intriguing *juvenilia*: his impressive account of Furness Abbey for the *Victoria History of the County of Lancashire* written in 1908, for instance; or his article, 'The Poetic in History', which appeared in October 1913 in the second volume of *History*, that 'indispensable magazine for teachers' as it boldly called itself in those hopeful days, and in which Powicke, equally boldly, discusses 'the poetic suggestiveness of history'; or (more relevant to our purpose) his paper entitled 'Boot and its Past', read to the Windscale Local History Society and published in its Transactions in January of the following momentous year.

In this *pièce d'occasion* Powicke draws attention to an omission which puzzled him and, once I had mastered my excitement at the association of St Penket with Boot, puzzled me also, but was to take me further along her trail. It is in a passage on the holy well at Boot that Powicke mentions St Penket, at first almost to my disbelief, for he drops her name into his discourse casually, as if his listeners – those few and earnest artisans of unspoilt Windscale – would know who she was. Here is the passage:

As late as the 1420s the well is called Penket's Well; women are said to have left garlands there in late May as gifts for the saint's aid in finding potent husbands and bearing sturdy children; one source suggests they danced with the garlands before putting them around the rim of the well. I have not been able to discover how this Staffordshire saint (who, incidentally, lived not a stone's throw from where today is the ground of the famous Stoke City Football Club) came to be associated with Eskdale. It is likely, I believe, that she came there on her way from Iona or Ireland. Perhaps she paused to perform a miracle, to overcome a heathen monster, or to provide some Christian relief to a hard-pressed pagan people, before moving on southwards. Yet famous as she once had been, by the 1420s her cult was surely near its end, for in the papal grant of parochial rights to St Catherine's chapel at Boot in 1445 neither she nor her well are mentioned. Possibly such popular manifestations of piety as I have described were too vulgar for the great men of the Church to notice or to deign to notice. Still, thereafter, although there are references to the holy well itself, there are no more to St Penket. It is as if she, or whatever it was which reminded people of her, had disappeared from Eskdale for ever between the 1420s and 1445.

Thus Powicke on St Penket in January 1914. Yet, if the trail had run cold for him, what chance had I of getting further on?

At this point I have to confess I had a stroke of luck. It consisted of one of those happy accidents upon which scholarship turns more often than scholars will readily admit: the fortuitous discovery in a calendar of documents taken from the shelf for some other, utterly different purpose, for example; or the decisive reference disclosed as one half-heartedly even aimlessly flicks through the card index in a County Record Office while waiting for an eagerly sought after document to appear, a document which turns out upon perusal to have made one's long and tedious journey unnecessary, were it not for that

chance discovery of another and fruitful reference.
In just such a haphazard fashion is the work of the
remainder of a lifetime set upon its unswerving
course. Where St Penket's leg and Boot are concerned, chance of just that sort was to play its part.

Before it did, it had crossed my mind, as no doubt
it has yours, that one unusual event which occurred
in the Lake District between the 1420s and 1445
was the visit in 1435–36 of Aeneas Sylvius Piccolo-
mini. That 30-year-old Italian nobleman, who in
1458 would become Pope Pius II and who has been
called 'a brilliant, genial and true spokesman of the
Renaissance', was in the winter of 1435–36 on his
way from Scotland, where he had been on embassy
to King James I and where (among other things) he
had permanently damaged his feet by walking bare-
foot in the snow for ten miles to give thanks to the
Blessed Virgin Mary for bringing him safely to land
after a stormy passage from the Low Countries, and
had fathered a son. The boy, like the other son he
had by a Breton woman – for the sophisticated
Aeneas appears to have made his more productive
conquests among the ladies of the remoter parts of
Christendom – died within a year or two of his birth,
perhaps fortunately for the later career of Aeneas: a
Scottish son of the Pope turning up at the Curia and
trying to make himself understood to his father may
have raised a few eyebrows even in that most
worldly of courts.

The Reverend Canon James Wilson has shown
conclusively in his paper, 'The passage of the Border
by Aeneas Sylvius in the winter of 1435–36', read at
Carlisle on 6th April 1922 to the Cumberland and
Westmoreland Antiquarian and Archaeological
Society, that Aeneas crossed the Solway Firth to
Bowness and then travelled east to Newcastle-on-
Tyne before going on to London, Dover and the short

channel crossing. His famous first night in England, therefore, was spent on the edge of the Lake District. I say 'famous', for this was the night Aeneas (disguised as a merchant) spent in a northern farming community. He describes in his Commentaries how everyone in the village came to stare at him (no doubt they had never seen an Italian disguised as a merchant before) and stayed to eat his white loaves and drink his red wine; then the men disappeared into the local peel tower in case the Scots should come, leaving Aeneas with the women; these, one hundred of them according to Aeneas, sat up talking for so long that he was too weary to accept the offer of the two who escorted him to his bed to join him in it. As he had to share his bed of straw with cows and goats, he got little sleep anyway. Next morning he set off for Newcastle.

All that is common knowledge and throws no light on St Penket's disappearance from Boot. Here, however, we arrive at my stroke of luck. I was investigating – for one of my classes on 'Religion and Art in the later Middle Ages' – Nicholas of Cusa, philosopher, theologian, mathematician, mystic, bishop, cardinal and reformer, in particular his emphasis on the visual as a mode of knowing God. His contemplative treatise *The Vision of God or the Icon*, for instance, is the only book of the Middle Ages (to my knowledge) to open with examples of contemporary painting. Nicholas and Aeneas were friends from the time they spent together at the Council of Basel; they died within three days of each other in August 1464. It was in one of the letters of Aeneas to Nicholas that I stumbled on what I had not been looking for. The letter is in an apparently somewhat obscure collection: 'Die Briefe des Aeneas Silvius vor seiner Erhebung auf den päpstlichen stuhl' in *Archiv für Kunde Österreichischer*

Geschichts-Quellen, Vol. 16 (Vienna, 1857). The letter's context is important.

In the summer of 1455 Aeneas was lobbying to become a cardinal, on this occasion, as it turned out, unsuccessfully. For this purpose he rallied his friends, among them the clever and influential cardinal Nicholas of Cusa. In 1455, Nicholas was close to completing one of the great charitable works of his life, his hospital for thirty-three poor men at Kues, his birthplace on the River Mosel; it was a work, as Aeneas well knew, on which Nicholas had set his heart; indeed, in 1464, Nicholas's heart would be buried in the chapel of his hospital. Aeneas appreciated, therefore, how to win or reinforce Nicholas's support for his candidature. I have rendered his flowery Renaissance Latin freely; my attempt to make it acceptable to us of the later twentieth century will not please everyone. Aeneas writes from Rome on 10th July 1455:

Knowing of your generous and renowned devotion to the cares of the old and afflicted, and understanding your worthy desire to receive the everlasting prayers of those whom your beneficent charity will provide for from among those bibulous old-timers of that delightful valley where the wine seems to flow even more liquidly than the river itself, or so on my visits it has seemed to me, I send you this holy armbone to adorn the altar of that chapel where each day on bended knee in numerical homage to their creator and in joyful remembrance of their founder these thirty-three decrepit Germans [*decrepiti et vetuli Teutonici*] will pray to the former to forgive the sins of the latter. It is the armbone of an ancient British saint [*antiquissima sancta Brittanorum*] whose chastity and virtuous life are testified to in many chronicles of that faithful Christian land and to whose abiding power I was witness when it saved me from gross and carnal sin. I was, dear Nicholas, alone with and encompassed by a multitude of the descendants of Eve, whose charms were abundant and abounding [*allicientiae copiosae et abundantes*] and whose husbands, brothers, sons and fathers were as far away as is the tavern of the Boat and Horses [*hosteria nomine bargettae et equorum nuncupata*] from the cathedral at Basel – do you remember Nicholas its snug back room? Yet, surrounded by the daughters of the Devil I, even I, was able by the strength of this bone which I had on a throng about my person to overcome all their temptations. To the bucolic bellowings of innocent beasts I fell into such a slumber that those lecherous northern peasants [*rusticae septentrionales impudicae*] could not disturb it. Such, my dear friend, you who have known me from the days of my zestful youth will understand was miraculous. Therefore, take this wonder-working bone; may she whose it is protect the aged inhabitants of your house of charity from those lusts which afflict the old even more than they do the young, for then they rot the mind more surely than they do the flesh, as long ago she protected both me and so many of her own sex. May our glorious Saviour ever have you in His keeping. . . .

Through this haze of self-regarding (and self-forgetting) twaddle we can clearly discern St Penket and, though it has become her arm, her leg.

Nevertheless, questions remain unanswered. What was St Penket's leg doing at Bowness about Christmas 1435? How had it got there from Boot? How had it become an arm? How did it get onto a throng around some part of the future Pius II's body? Had he given anything for it, if so what? Or, had he stolen it? Moreover, can we be sure it was a bone of St Penket? I mean, even if we assume Aeneas's *antiquissima sancta Brittanorum* was St Penket, and I think we should, would he have given to Nicholas the relic which he maintained had kept him from sexual intercourse with any number (from two to a hundred) of lusty northern women in the

depths of a northern winter? Would he not have kept
it and sent Nicholas a counterfeit from some Roman
refuse dump or other? Of course, we cannot know.
We have to assume that he was as good as his word.
After all, Renaissance fraud though he was, would
Aeneas have cheated where such matters were concerned? I believe we have to accept, that we *can*
accept – as I immediately accepted, or if I may
suggest it intuitively recognized, on reading
Aeneas's letter – that St Penket's leg was indeed the
arm which Aeneas believed had saved him from a
night's wrestling with Cumberland ladies and which
on 10th July 1455 he sent to Nicholas of Cusa's
hospital at Kues.

Even as we accept that, however, we are bound to
ask, as I was quick to ask myself, how does St
Penket's leg, having been duly placed in a modified
thirteenth-century arm reliquary, thereafter kept in
the hospital chapel, get from Kues to Birmingham
via the dealer Barling? The short answer is that I
know how it left Kues because I was there or
thereabouts when it was stolen on 13th August
1955, the five-hundredth anniversary to the day of
its ceremonial and celebratory arrival at Kues. The
longer answer is the final episode in this story of St
Penket's leg and Boot.

What happened first after my discovery of
Aeneas's letter was my remembering where I had
seen the Birmingham reliquary before. The recollection was sudden and complete. I had no doubts. It
came as I was looking on the map for Kues, and
having found it saw that at no great distance from it
lay Traben-Trarbach. For it was at Traben-Trarbach
that I had seen the reliquary. Looking up my journal
I found when: 13th August 1955, a memorable day
in my life as on the evening of it I underwent a rite
of passage which every western European man

undergoes. I got drunk for the first time. My inebriation, however, was not the reason for my not recognizing the reliquary for what it was when I saw it in 1955: as a priggish 18-year-old Protestant, stone-cold sober I would have had no idea what a reliquary was. Yet although that night I may not have known what a reliquary was, it had been such an evening of vivid impressions I had retained a clear, even a photographic image of it. After all, whatever the circumstances and however you are feeling, if you open your sleeping bag to reveal a more than life-size, silver-gilt thirteenth-century hand your memory of it is likely to be good.

How did it get there? I had my suspicions. When I wrote to my former German pen-friend with whom I was staying in 1955 and who had been my companion in Traben-Trarbach he replied confirming them. His father had died in the late 1960s; he had, therefore, no cause to keep silent and no reason to lie about yet another extraordinary exploit of that imaginative and enterprising man. Klaus Kellermann was a dashing and direct inside-forward in the German football team which played England in Berlin in May 1938 and a tank regiment captain in June 1940 who urged similar tactics at Dunkirk, which if they had been adopted by his superiors might have resulted in disaster for the British army and thus perhaps for the British people. He retained his belief in the destiny of the German nation under Adolf Hitler up to and beyond the end of the war in 1945. By the time I encountered him and his family in Cologne ten years later he was a genial but impressive businessman, whose business I never quite understood. These days his involvement in many of the money-raising ventures which financed the escape of senior members of the Nazi party to South America is well known, though what exactly

his part was in the forging and sale of the Vinland
Map will perhaps never be known. His son believes
he took a leading role in the affair. Possibly his
geniality in the summer of 1955 was not uncon-
nected with the sizeable remuneration and intellectual satisfaction such a perfect deception of the
academic world had brought him. Probably it also
had a good deal to do with the adventure he was
preparing while I was there: the theft of the Kues
hospital reliquary. With his nice sense of occasion
Herr Kellermann, who knew his Rhineland history
with a professional thoroughness only to be expected
in a German amateur, had chosen the anniversary
of its coming to the hospital to be the time of its
departure. His tidy-mindedness was also patriotic;
five hundred years in one place, his son told me, his
father considered long enough: it was high time
reliquary and relic began to help Germans in a more
modern fashion.

Thus, when we set off in the brown Volkswagen
for our camping trip into the Taunus hills by way of
Traben-Trarbach the date as well as the details of
der Reliquienkästchenlichen Raubzug (as his son
has termed it in his letter to me) had been determined. Why else, I ask now, should we have been
travelling to the Taunus by way of Traben-
Trarbach? It was not apparently a difficult job as
these affairs go; indeed, as his son writes, for his
nerveless father it was *ein Stück Kuchen*. While the
rest of us were drinking Mosel in Traben-Trarbach
Herr Kellermann had driven over the intervening
hill and down into Bernkastel. There he had met his
accomplices and they had slipped across the river to
Kues. It was a warm, moonless night; there was an
inside man (a former parachute sergeant-major, now
the porter and caretaker); the watchdogs had been
drugged; the doors unlocked; the reliquary was in an

21

open case in the sacristy; it was soon *im Sack*: in the bag. Within the hour St Penket's leg was in another sort of bag, the one in which I was to sleep, and Herr Kellermann was back with us in the restaurant. I, well lubricated, barely registered his return. He had made only one error: he had put the reliquary in the wrong sleeping bag. It was not a fatal mistake, merely a tiny flaw in this otherwise flawless operation of a perfectionist. He had omitted to ask which of the two sleeping bags his son was to sleep in. His wrong choice did not matter. Immediately after I had discovered the reliquary in my sleeping bag I had (in reaching out for support in my unsteady state) broken the ridge pole of the tent. This did not perturb me, but in the confusion of sagging canvas and a swaying inebriate the reliquary was transferred; when I fell into the sleeping bag shortly afterwards it had gone. It never entered my mind again until I saw it in Birmingham over twenty years later.

The remainder of the story is quickly told. The shadowy art dealer Barling was contacted at his book-lined home in Düsseldorf. There was a meeting in the Pinkus-Müller home brew house in that city, to which the secretive and eccentric Barling is reported to have gone on a bicycle. A deal was done and the reliquary changed hands there and then. A few years later it was in the Barber Institute.

Of this remarkable history – for to call it remarkable is not, I believe, extravagant – I have a memento: a photograph of our tent by the Mosel on an August morning in 1955. Inside the tent is St Penket's leg. It had come a long way from Penkhull. This snapshot now adorns my desk, a reminder of the occasion when my prosaic destiny for a brief

summer's night crossed that of one of the greatest of
Celtic saints.

This is the text of an illustrated lecture given to the Humanities
Society at the Teesside Polytechnic on 23rd March 1984.

3

A William Sponne Deed at Towcester: further light on the cult of St Penket.

The facts of history are bad enough; the fictions are, if possible, worse.

Henry James, *A Little Tour in France*
(1884, reprinted 1984) p 35.

ONCE upon a time I worked for Princess Diana's grandfather. That time was twenty-five years ago this summer. I celebrated the anniversary by returning to the Northamptonshire countryside which I had got to know (and love) in the summer of 1959. Then I cycled about it; this summer I motored through it: such is the measure of the decline of the West. My journey turned out to be more than nostalgic; it produced an historical discovery of almost dreamlike dimensions. This discovery I wish to share with you.

Let me delay that revelation and keep you for a little in suspense while I set it in the context not only of this summer but also of that summer of twenty-five years ago. For I know you are asking yourselves what kind of work was he doing for the fifth Earl Spencer?

It had been arranged by a history tutor at the University of Leicester that I should sort out and list the documents in the muniment room at Althorp. Not the important documents I hasten to add; those had all been catalogued and boxed: the sheep accounts of the sixteenth century, the letters of Nelson and others to the Spencer lord of the Admiralty during the Napoleonic Wars, the Red Earl's papers (indispensible for the history of Ireland and the Liberal Party at the close of the nineteenth century), and the notebooks in cipher of the Honourable Francis Spencer (plain Frank or F.S. to his friends), a British agent in the German Grand Fleet and one of the instigators of the mutiny at Wilhelmshaven in August 1917. These precious papers resided in an orderly *inner sanctum*. To get to it you went through four other rooms where tin and cardboard boxes once arranged were now in disarray, and where bundles of documents and loose papers lay about, having been taken out and never having been replaced. They were overwhelmingly deeds and estate vouchers of the eighteenth and nineteenth centuries. My humble, proletarian task was to tidy up, put into order, label and list the contents of these four rooms. It seemed fairly daunting but I had three months to do it in and (to my relief) I was left alone to do it. In these days of the professional, a raw and unqualified graduate would not be allowed to tamper freely with what the fifth Earl, a committed private owner who considered himself a trustee for everything that had been handed down to him, regarded as a precious heritage. Possibly even in those days, such a tyro would not, or ought not to have been hired; the fifth Earl, however, was a parsimonious man: he had a great house, a large

park and numerous farms to run, some remarkable
possessions to care for and a place in society to
maintain; cheap labour was what he required.

Actually, not so cheap. Originally it had been
intended that I should stay at Althorp itself, but an
apologetic letter had reached me before I departed
for Northmaptonshire: as the married Italian couple
who were his man-servant and Lady Spencer's maid-
servant would be returning to their homeland for
the greater part of the summer, Earl Spencer regret-
ted that I could not be looked after properly at
Althorp; therefore he had booked me into the local
inn, the Red Lion at East Haddon, which would
provide dinner as well as a proper breakfast. At the
Red Lion I lived like a lord nonetheless; frequently
the only guest, I would dine in noble isolation off the
cook's finest. This was at great cost to the Earl; the
landlord showed me the bill that was sent to him; I
was charged for every bath I took, overcharged on
every meal I ate. Because it was so expensive to keep
me in such an unaccustomed fashion, Lord Spencer
paid me a pittance. I remonstrated with him, told
him he was being diddled. To no effect: he was
immovable. Was this how a gentleman behaved, or
did he simply not want me in his house? While I
pondered the unfair ways of this unfamiliar world
the beneficiary of the Earl's quaint manners and
queer economics was the landlord of the Red Lion.

Not that I did not get on with him. Indeed, as a
resident (which meant I could drink a quenching
pint when I got back after the mainly uphill cycle
ride from Althorp, three or more miles distant),
shortly I was so much 'part of the place' that
sometimes I served behind the bar and frequently
pulled my five-thirty pint for myself. So accepted did
I become that I was allowed to observe (as Lord
Spencer's salary did not allow me to play in) the

small and select after-hours gambling school which functioned on Saturday nights. On one such night, after I had sat enthralled to see a *nouveau riche* from Northampton drunkenly wager and lose £40 in less than two minutes, it was I (a relatively sober and uninvolved bystander – rather like one of Professor Peter Brown's holy men on the edge of society yet essential to it) who was detailed to go out to recover the unlucky punter from the inky night into which he had rushed distraught. I found him in a telephone kiosk; how I talked him into returning I cannot remember. Of course, I also drank too much, though given my paltry wage only once memorably; the next morning I awoke in a wardrobe where, apparently upright, I had spent the night. As the last thing I recalled doing the previous evening was quietly reading Carlyle's *French Revolution* in the public bar this came as a distinct surprise.

My other memories are of the landscape I cycled through to work each day – Saturday mornings too I may add, for I was following Public Record Office procedure– or went out into at weekends: those Northamptonshire Heights as geographers call that rolling countryside through which the M1 did not then sweep, though I remember crossing the brown gash its making had already imposed on the landscape. Village cricket too I recollect, watching not playing; the harvest coming in; my early evening walk beyond the western end of the village; Brixworth church with a wedding just ended; above all, the servants of Althorp and Wednesday afternoons, when visitors were shown round the house by a lady from the village, Great Brington on the hill: Althorp having been eaten up by sheep as early as 1500. The estimable Mr. Crook, the Butler, sat at the entrance collecting the visitors' money; the Earl hovered, every now and again pouncing out fiercely from

some secret door or other to startle and shout at
people for fingering his treasures. There were many
of these; even in what had been the servants' rooms
in the attics there were Edward Lear landscapes;
these the public never saw. Lord Spencer let me
show them to my friends, but not to my parents
when they came to carry me away at the end of my
labours, for like a jack-in-the-box he had popped up
in the library to catch my father with his hand on a
valueless nineteenth-century globe of the world, and
that was the end of the tour. The library (its wonder-
ful paintings apart) was the saddest room at
Althorp: its choice collection of manuscripts and
early printed books had departed to become the
basis of the John Rylands Library at Manchester.
Like the Holbein portrait of Henry VIII, sold to the
Thyssen-Bornemisza collection at Lugano in the
1930s to raise death duties, the former contents of
the library were a gap in his heirlooms which the
fifth Earl Spencer never ceased to regret.

He had a splendid memory. He would, if he was on
his own, summon me to take afternoon tea with him.
This was not a notable event, so far as the food went
– from the fact that the Earl's favourite dish was
Irish stew you can judge that I was decidedly better
off eating at the Red Lion than I would have been
feeding in this nobleman's household – but it was for
the stories he told, like the uncomplimentary ones of
the Prince of Wales in the First World War, or those
revealing Winston Churchill's unwinning ways
when he came to stay between the wars, or that of
the duel between Sir Oswald Mosley and Dame
Edith Sitwell, fought at Christmas 1931, or the one
about the notorious party held in the summer house
by Frank Spencer before he left to join the Secret
Service, and even some of the great Red Earl, who
had what he regarded as a playful habit but the

children saw as a frightening trick of hiding from them in the space dividing the double doors that there were between many downstairs rooms. Normally I ate with the servants: Cook at one end of the table, Mr. Crook at the other, the rest of us arranged hierarchically between them. Sometimes, if the Earl and Countess had visitors, I would join them for lunch in the small and exquisite dining room; I suppose I was being shown off, although precisely as what I am reluctant to think. That was how I encountered the Earl's son Viscount Althorp and his children. The realisation came as a shock (when the Prince of Wales' engagement was announced) that Princess Diana had not yet been one of them. If she had been, I would have been poor company for her. I was a morose youth. It was a curious summer. As my journal of it shows.

What, for instance, should one make of the following entry for 10 August:

> G. talks about the seven men and the seven worlds arising from the law of threes. Men one, two and three are surely almost equal in development, or at least more nearly equal than man three is to man four. O. remarks somewhere in *Tertium Organum* that all men are governed by emotion in the end. Anyway that does not matter very much because all three types (present in each individual) must be collectively crystallized, as they are in man four, before any progress can begin. I pray that I stand within the ray of creation and that I have not wasted my energy or will continue to waste it so that work will not be able to begin on the self because it is enervated.

Or this (and it shall be the last I will inflict on you):

> Fred G. wrote. He confirms the fourth way is the only way. Yet how far are material and external conditions stifling of any concentrated development of the whole consciousness? I tend to think after six years of formal

THE PENKET PAPERS

training of the mind only of the intellect: here also one
is hampered. The body, the emotions, the will are all
overlooked or ignored. How to develop these and the
consciousness when one is surrounded and concerned
by unreal events and everyday ideas? The fourth way is
thus the hardest way.

Yes, you have guessed: I was going through my
Ouspenskian phase. G. is Gurdjieff whose unread-
able *All and Everything* I had not then read; when I
did so later, in a foolhardy endeavour to combat the
horrors of the University of Oxford which thrust
themselves upon me the following autumn, I joined
that select band of those who have managed to reach
the last of its 1238 pages of timelessly arcane drivel.
Fred G. shall remain anonymous. His penniless
descent upon provincial Leicester with his news of
Ouspenskian groups in the metropolis – The Work
as they were mystifying called – seemed fabulous
and was fabulously disturbing, for he appeared as I
was about to take Finals. That was no time to go in
search of the miraculous, as at least one of my
examiners made clear when she refused to give any
mark at all to one of my papers. I was still searching
in Northamptonshire later in the summer. There
are sorrowful entries in my journal: I find the
octaves almost impossible to understand; having
looked at the table of hydrogens I am near to
faintheartedness; the table of cosmoses I do not
follow. These suggest that the seeker was not
finding a great deal. Developing the whole consciousness was a grim business and I must have
been joyless company. A prude as well as prune, for I
discover that I considered 'Some Like it Hot' a
'cheap, nasty and usually unfunny film'. Still, I was
able to notch up my second mystical experience
(about midnight on 13 September), and you will be
equally pleased to learn there is this entry on 24

31

August: 'I heard today that I had been awarded a
state studentship. This [the laconic entry goes on
and concludes] was a relief'. As it meant I would go
to Oxford instead of into the Army Medical Corps I
suppose it must have been. Moreover, on 2 September there is a passionate note that carries convic-
tion: 'With the subjunctive Latin becomes difficult'.
It seems I had not entirely given up mundane
pursuits. The miraculous was held a little at bay.

My other reading – Salinger and Ibsen, Camus
and Sartre – cannot have done much to lighten the
gloom. Yet, beside the effusive nonsense I poured
out after seeing Ibsen's 'Brand' on television on 11
August, I discern the shape of things to come in my
note of another television programme on 25 August:
'A Carmelite abbey in Wales. The nuns were
radiant; there is no other word to describe their joy,
peace and delicacy of speech and manner'. Is there a
faint trace here of my one day being able to grasp
(albeit dimly still) that the universe might revolve
around others than myself? As I take leave of this
catalogue of self-pity, you will be relieved that in
three months I did have one moment of what I called
'ease' – evidently I could not bring myself to write
'happiness'. It was while returning to Northampton
on a bus and coming through Brixworth at dusk
with the pub doors open and their windows lit up.
For me such moments continue to be, as the sight
and sound of mixed choral music is too, a glimpse
into paradise. You will also be relieved to know that
as soon as this sentence was written my solipsist
journal (a glance into hell perhaps) was destroyed.

Such nostalgia for the summer of 1959, which I
carried with me into Northamptonshire in the summer of 1984, was for absolutely nothing set out in
that diary of the absurd. What overwhelmed me now
was the beauty of the countryside (barely noticed in

my self-absorption of twenty-five years before) and
its current well-being, not seen at all if it existed
then but seen clearly now, coming as I was this time
from the North, not as a quarter of a century before
from the South. After a blazing morning at Weedon
Lois with its holy well of St Loy, Slapton with its
delightful wall-paintings, and Grafton Regis, where
Edward IV had married Elizabeth Woodvill and
where now rampant nettles covered whatever traces
they might have left, I arrived at Towcester at lunch
time. In the afternoon I would drive across the
motorway to Great Brington, Althorp and East
Haddon.

Towcester was a surprise. I half-expected to encounter a steam train in its vicinity so abruptly and
thoroughly was I cast back into the 1950s. After the
lush affluence of the morning's villages, where in
every tasteful conversion and each freshly painted
extension the smug manifestation of one of the two
nations Mrs. Thatcher has created since 1979 (this
one at the expense of the other) seemed to be
revealed, Towcester, while neither shabby nor down
at heel, appeared at once part of an earlier, better
world. Its High Street bustled but not impatiently.
Here was time to spare. People looked like characters, especially in the welcoming shadiness of the
bar of The Saracen's Head; entering it on such a day
of light and heat was like diving underwater. I knew
it had featured in *The Pickwick Papers*; it remained,
thank God, Pickwickian. I took my glass of shandy,
sparkling in the sunshine, into the innyard. Con-
ning my Pevsner I learned there were two things I
should see: the cinema of brick of 1939, built by Lord
Hesketh for his wife as a birthday present (it had a
private family box), and in the church the tomb of
William Sponne, the town's benefactor, founder of
chantry and school, archdeacon of Norfolk from

33

1419, rector at Towcester from 1422, who had died in 1448.

It was no distance from pub to church, merely the length of the short High Street. In its enclosed and grassy yard, like others from offices, shops and banks, I ate my sandwiches. I was anticipating no more surprises. Nor at first, when I went into the church did I come across any. William Sponne lay newly painted in lively effigy above; William Sponne as rotting corpse lay starkly below. I stood reflecting: was he the image, the double image of our divided nation? I dismissed this portentous thought and turning away noticed hung and framed upon the wall beside him a document. It turned out to be an indenture of the release by William to his chantry priests of plate and vestments for their use on the altar in this south aisle of Towcester church. It was signed as well as sealed by William and was dated 5 November 1447, a couple of months after, as I subsequently discovered, he had made his will.

It appeared to be unremarkable: the liturgical objects were unspectacular, the transaction straightforward. Nevertheless, out of professional habit and because once before at Dennington in Suffolk, where beside the resplendent fifteenth-century tomb of William Philip, lord Bardolf and his wife I had found on the obverse of a Bardolf chantry document, similarly displayed, a Phillipps Collection mark which I was able to communicate to A.N.L. Munby for his famous catalogue, I took the frame from the wall and turned it over. The frame was backed. I hesitated. Should I bother? Ought I to? There was no one in the church; the sunlight flooded in; a fly buzzed in the emptiness. I hesitated no longer. The clips holding in the backing board presented little difficulty; I lifted it away and placed it against the foot of the tomb. There was no backing paper or cardboard, simply the reverse of the document itself. On it was writing, what looked to me like three stanzas of a poem, tidily written; only in a very few places were there crossings out and interlineations. I read the fifteenth-century hand with mounting excitement; as I reached the end of the third stanza I slumped into a chair: my state was one of trembling astonishment. So much for no more surprises (was the thought which came to my head). Yet surprised, staggered indeed as I had been, my condition was not one of shock. Careless now of whether anyone came to interrupt me, I took out pencil and notebook and transcribed the three stanzas. I took my time, folk came and went but not one of them disturbed me. Satisfied at last with my transcription I replaced the indenture in its frame and hung it again upon the wall. I reeled out into the sunny churchyard, sat on the grass, my back against a tombstone, and contemplated the following:

Nowe herken gentle yemen
Of our brave Robyn Hode
How he gat john of Oxenford
In Bernsdale to doo sum gode.

Yore eryng and sowyng are ore
Yore hervest ys yet to bee done
Soo reste from yemanly taskes
And lye on the grene yn the sunne.

Hear me alle you good fremen
Tell of Robyns sumer banqete
Of the dancyng in the grene wode
Yn honore of holi Penkete.

These verses, I think, speak for themselves and are more than adequate explanation of the excitement which I have described. I should, however, add that while there is no doubt whatsoever about the names Penket, John of Oxenford, Barnsdale and Robin

Hood, my reading of the word banquet, with which the writer (or possibly the author) had difficulty also as he made two attempts at it, might be disputed. Yet what else could it be is a question I have often, as you may imagine, asked myself. I have said 'Possibly the author', but is it likely that the archdeacon of Norfolk composed these verses? They are, as my immediate comparison with his signature on the obverse of the indenture at once showed, in his hand. I believe too that there were three other stanzas and that they are or were to be found on the other, William's part of the indenture. That was evident from the manner in which the surviving three stanzas were set out on the paper and the form of its indented edge. William, therefore, had used for the indenture of 5 November 1447 the reverse of a sheet of paper on which he had previously copied out (or composed) the first six stanzas of a Robin Hood ballad. Would this not have been an unusually informal approach to the transaction the indenture embodied? Perhaps William Sponne was that sort of man, perhaps the handing over of the plate and vestments was done in a rush when there was no clean parchment or paper to hand, but the sheet with the Robin Hood verses on it. Or perhaps both.

William was a Cambridge graduate, a former steward of John Wakering, bishop of Norwich, and no doubt like his patron he was a vigorous, knowledgeable man; there is nothing in his career to suggest he would not have paper about the house, or that he sat around composing Robin Hood ballads, even, for that matter, merely transcribing them. Yet who knows? At the end of his life (he was dead by February 1448), like Thomas Aquinas he may have had a change of heart, a sudden stroke of deeper understanding, a flash of illumination, in which it was revealed that there was more to life than being

an archdeacon: there was poetry too. That he may
have been odd in his last days is indicated by the
discovery after his death of items of gold and silver
hidden in a wall of the parsonage at Towcester. Also,
in his will he made a special point of his bequests of
money to the ploughmen, that is (I take it), the
husbandmen of that town. Are there connections to
be made here between a preoccupation with Robin
Hood, the stowing away of valuables, a concern for
the yeomen and husbandmen of England, and William's carelessness about protocol? It would be fanci-
ful to speculate further.

For me, for us indeed, it is the appearance in these
verses of St Penket which is significant. The connection of her with dancing might have been unnerv-
ing, were it not for the growing volume of evidence
(which I have not yet published) of her fame –
greater, interestingly enough, in the Islamic world
than in Christendom – as a whirling, dancing saint.
Much turns upon – I almost said revolves upon – a
suitably gnomic Anglo-Saxon riddle which has recently come to light. I am in no doubt that she was
an early exponent of a mystical tradition, the ecstatic dance, which never developed within Western
Christianity. I consider the medieval accounts of
women dancing in springtime around the holy well
associated with her at Boot in Cumbria conclusive.
Penket, I am sure, was honoured in Northern England at that time of the year and in a manner
appropriate to her attribute: the dance. There is
more to be said on this; I shall say it elsewhere.
What William Sponne's verses demonstrate is that
such honour, in name at least, was still being paid
her in another part of England in the later Middle
Ages. Moreover, even if her name occurs merely for
the sake of the rhyme, which I cannot believe
(though banquet I admit *is* a hard word to rhyme),

that testified nonetheless to there being some life left after so many centuries. Probably she was far more important than that, for it may be that she had had a role to play (and as a dancer this would be understandable) in the evolution of the May Games. The revolving around a central, fixed point, the May Pole, is suggestive, although (alas) I have not so far come across a Penket Pole. Was not Penket Maid Marion's predecessor in the May Games? When, one wonders, did one replace the other as Robin's partner in that springtime dancing? Was it on the eve of the Reformation? Have we here a small but telling segment of that secularization of society – as historians term the accumulation of such trivial transformations – which was, if not the cause, the essential precondition of the religious revolution of the sixteenth century?

Important as William Sponne's verses are for our growing awareness of the cult of a forgotten saint, they are no less vital for the historian's understanding and interpretation of the Robin Hood legends. I am less than expert in the critical controversy which has arisen over the origin of the legends and their audience, but while our paltry three stanzas, undoubtedly opening ones, do not reveal much about the nature of the legends, even I can see that they contain a few clues as to the legends' origin and audience. Are these convincing clues? I doubt it. For two reasons: the late date of our source on the one hand, and on the other the fact that controversalists by definition are unable to accept that controversy, their controversy at any rate, should cease. Yet the naming of a well-documented sheriff of Nottingham of the 1330s has surely to count for something in the debate over the legends' origins. And the equally marvellous (I almost said miraculous) naming of the tasks of yeomen so transparently not those of servingmen is surely the sort of gift-horse one side in the controversy about the ballads' audience would not wish to look in the mouth. Nor, so far as I am able to see, is the line 'And lye on the grene yn the sunne' any less unequivocal: there is from such a vantage point not a baronial hall in sight. I will leave matters there and let others who are expert in these issues explore the decisiveness of what is, however you approach it, a revealing new source.

Such then was my good fortune on a hot summer's day in Towcester in 1984. As you may imagine, my return to Althorp later that afternoon had an air of anti-climax about it. Of course, I drew immense pleasure from my visit, far more than I did from my early evening pint at the refurbished and virtually unrecognisable Red Lion at East Haddon. Althorp had changed much less. Still, I was, I have to admit, preoccupied, until I recalled the one discovery of interest I had made there twenty-five years before. In the room furthest from the well-known and well-used treasures of the central muniment room, in a box to the back and high up on a shelf almost out of sight and out of mind, I came upon a clutch of pathetic letters from a woman whose illegitimate baby by a young mid-nineteenth-century Spencer had died. He too had died, killed in the Crimea, though not before he had filled a notebook with sketches of a high quality. The wronged woman's letters to the family, ever more incoherent and at last plumb crazy, went on almost to the end of the century. My sudden recollection of this old Spencer skeleton in the cupboard made me chuckle because of the moment at which it had come. For now it was a skeleton I would never let out: Princess Diana must be allowed to continue to live happily ever after. Besides, I had in my pocket – and I patted the place where my transcription of the Robin Hood verses nestled snugly – evidence if not to dish, at least to embarrass an only slightly less distinguished and undoubtedly more learned member of the English Establishment, a man you have by this time certainly identified, that is, the President of the Royal Historical Society.

This paper was read at Florence Boot Hall, Nottingham University on 20 September 1984.

4

Nineteen-Fourteen

'I am unbound
Twisting and turning
Around
Whirling to the sounds.'

(From the tenth-century Crediton Riddle Book)

I

THEY sat at a table in Schmidts, Charlotte Street. It
was lunchtime on a Friday in January. Their table
was on the first floor by the window of a long narrow
room. Outside, the pale sunshine lit up the busy
street; inside, cutlery shone on starched white tab-
lecloths. They were served by the waiter Henry had
come to know well. 'How's your brother's new bak-
ery Alfred?', Henry asked him as he brought their
Kaiserrippchen. At a table nearby sat two young
men artistically dressed. 'Do you know them?', Marcel inquired of Henry, shovelling *sauerkraut* onto his
plate. Henry paused before replying to note how
little *sauerkraut* remained for his portion; he raised
his eyebrows at this manifestation of his friend's

41

Gallic appetite. 'The ugly one is called Stanley Spencer, the handsome one John Currie.' Henry applied mustard to his pork. 'Is there no French mustard?', asked Marcel. 'No', replied Henry, with a greater satisfaction than he felt he ought to have displayed, 'only German'. He preferred the colour as well as the taste, he thought, looking across to observe Currie gesticulating extravagantly. Curious, their laden forks between plate and open mouth, Henry and Marcel caught the names Duchamp and Kupka in Currie's passionate discourse and watched Spencer shaking his head. 'My Cookham feelings', he interjected suddenly, 'are really that I feel this Ascot Fashion Boulters Lock Sunday Bank Holiday Terrific Physical Life can be so tremendous seen spiritually, and this desire on my part is intensified by the fact that Cookham has, so far as nature aspects are concerned and as far as different jobs that are done there, an affinity with the Bible. So that all the things that happen at Cookham happen in the Bible. Isn't cow parsley as much part of the Gospel story as the words and sufferings of Jesus?'. Currie dipped his spoon into his *creme caramel*. 'Have you seen my Penkhull?', he responded. 'Oh, and Stanley you should see Frank's Nini among Verticals'. The young man waved his spoon, narrowly missing Alfred who was returning with an additional dish of *sauerkraut* for Henry. Spencer, oblivious of this, exclaimed, 'But my John Donne arriving in Heaven John, didn't you understand that? Ah, I do want to paint JC and Co like a football team, don'tcha know, sitting there in two rows with their arms folded like this and looking tough'. Currie laughed, 'Millwall are at home tomorrow Stan, we'll go to the Den and then you'll see how tough they look'. Spencer knit his brows. 'But you can see that John can't you, that there's nothing pointless in the notion of saints watching boys playing marbles?.' 'Or boys watching saints for that matter, I suppose,' said Currie reaching into his waistcoat pocket and pulling out his watch. 'Come on Stanley, we should have been at Dolly's half an hour ago.' Watching the two hoisting themselves into their overcoats, Marcel pondered on the sort of marbles saints might play with, while Henry turned over the word Penkhull in his mind. Wasn't it the painting he had seen over Arnold Bennett's fireplace?. And wasn't it more than that? Hadn't there been resonances even then, as he had admired the picture and Bennett had pronounced, with a note of apology in his voice, the name? He was roused from his musings by the waiter at his elbow. 'Some *Emmentaler* I think, Alfred.' he decided. Marcel clicked his tongue. He wanted to be off to the Tower of London.

Ravens stalked the grass outside the Lieutenant's Lodging and the warders were in their winter capes. Henry had shown Marcel the prisoners' vigorous graffiti in the Beauchamp Tower and he had been interested in Thomas Abell's Bell and the story Henry had told him of the martyrs of 1540, protestant and catholic on each hurdle ecumenically drawn to Tyburn to satisfy Henry VIII's equally ecumenical tyranny. Now they stared at the spot where his wives had suffered. Henry intoned his fellow countryman's lines,

'Tudor indeed is gone and every rose,
Blood-red, blanch-white that in the sunset glows
Cries: 'Blood, Blood, Blood!' against the gothic stone
Of England, as the Howard or Boleyn knows.'

Marcel snorted and stalked away. He admired neither the history the lines gave expression to nor the manner in which they expressed it. Henry followed him across to the chapel of St. Peter Ad Vincula. The rosy-cheeked warder let them in and was soon declaiming to them and a handful of other visitors what the 1876 commission had discovered beneath the pavement. 'Two thousand bodies, and only thirty-three of them identifiable, ladies and gentlemen.' Henry was moved. 'Doesn't that give you a sense of the past of this place, Marcel?' he commented as they walked slowly over to the White Tower. Marcel halted, his hand on Henry's arm, 'Henry,' he said, 'if we wish to retain some freshness of impressions, some creative power, the wisdom of that Muse must be ignored as long as possible. But even those who have ignored her meet her in the evening of their lives in the nave of an old country church, at a point when suddenly they feel less susceptible to the eternal beauty expressed in the carvings on the altar than to the thought of the vicissitude of fortune which those carvings have undergone.' He disengaged his hand and they continued. 'But what of the feel of the stopped pulse, the tick of old stopped clocks?' It was Henry's turn to pause and choose his words. 'I suppose she cannot give us that, those little notes of truth which, however she might bury her nose, she cannot discover. You and I want evidence of a kind for which there aren't documents enough or for which documents, however multiplied, would never be enough.' He dug his finger into Marcel's ribs: 'Thats our method – to try for an ell in order to get an inch.' Marcel winced. He was getting cold. 'Let us walk back through the City', he said. Isn't a frivolous theme though as good as any other, he asked himself as they picked their way fastidiously along Lower Thames Street and past the Monument. A fishporter may serve for a study of the laws of character as well as any saint, Captain Blood do as well as Captain Scott. He was

lost in thought all the way to the churchyard of St.
Botolph, Aldersgate.

Henry was reading out the plaques. 'Frederick
Alfred Croft, inspector aged thirty-one, saved a
lunatic woman from suicide at Woolwich Arsenal
station but was himself run over by the train. Alice
Ayres, daughter of a bricklayer's labourer, who by
intrepid conduct saved three children from a burn-
ing house in Union Street Borough at the cost of her
own young life. Arthur Strange, carman of London,
and Mark Tomlinson on a desperate venture to save
two girls from a quicksand in Lincolnshire were
themselves engulfed. Ernest Benning, compositor
aged twenty-two, upset from a boat one dark night
off Pimlico Pier grasped an oar with one hand
supporting a woman with the other but sank as she
was rescued.' The low, red sun illumined the coloured tiles of the inscriptions. Henry was quoting
again: 'a golden bowl full of incense made of the
prayers of the saints.' Marcel gazed at the glazed
memorial tablets. This was a nation of Oates. What
was it that sergeant at Doncières who had been on
Devil's Island had asked him: how many pages did
he think he might fill describing the perturbation of
a human soul placed in a cell filled to twenty times
its capacity, with no latrine bucket and where the
prisoners were taken out to the lavatory only once a
day? The dilemma of whether to urinate in your
canvas hat or your canvas shoe. Wouldn't such a
work be like that written 'On the Backs of National
Gallery Pictures'? He thought not. That pail which
wasn't – might it not be as much a foundation stone
of a life as for him had been the sight of the steeples
of Martinville? He sighed. Henry was leading him
out of the churchyard and telling him of the three
things which were important in human life. The
first, he said, was to be kind, the second was to be

kind, and the third was to be kind. Walking past St.
Pauls, which in the dusk was shining out at every
window and seemed to expand with the life within
it, Marcel wondered if he might not combine two
things that had never existed together before; they
could then begin a new existence and so enrich the
spheres. Henry was still talking, telling him now
about a pit disaster. In Durham 164 men had been
entombed. When their bodies had been discovered,
written on a roof plank there had also been found
these words, 'The Lord has been with us. We are
ready for heaven. Bless the Lord. We have had a
jolly prayer meeting. Every man is ready for glory.'
How, Marcel wondered, did such a singularly and
patently moral man write such intricately woven
fables of good and evil? They had arrived at the inky
river. People were milling into a station.

Henry and Marcel entered the saloon bar of The
Blackfriar. Around them city gentlemen were drinking whiskies and sodas. Before long they would be
home in Denmark Hill, Nunhead or Brockley, the
fire which had recently toasted tea for their children
welcoming their return to middle-class insecurity.
Henry and Marcel took their pints of guinness to the
snug where below fat friars in bronze they encountered an Italian-looking man with a glass of gin and
angustura bitters in front of him. He was as startled
as they were and quickly emptying his glass he
departed. 'Wasn't that Domenico Antonio Iannetti?',
Henry enquired of Marcel. Marcel nodded. An evening in Venice returned to him. The twilit water
patterning the ceiling, the lapping of that same
water against the villa wall below the open window.
Domenico singing. The taste of almonds. The scent
of roses. Yes, the true paradises were the paradises
we had lost. Or, were they the ones we had never
found? Or, the ones we would never even seek?

Marcel's reverie was interrupted by Henry's reminding him it was his round. 'What is he doing in London at this time of the year?', Henry asked him as he returned with their drinks. What indeed. Was his presence in London linked with the previous day's sale of a fourteenth-century manuscript of the Discourses of Jalal al-Din Rumi which had recently turned up in a junk shop in Crewe? Henry seemed to have lost interest in Iannetti almost immediately he had taken him up and opened *The Times* which lay on the table Iannetti had the moment before vacated. 'I see,' he said after perusing it for a while, 'that they've put the Middlesbrough Meteorite on show in the Yorkshire Museum'. He drank from his glass and returned behind the paper. A page turned. 'And, you know, this Millie Marley sect seems to be growing; it says here that another two girls have been charged by the North Yorkshire police at Yarm.' The saloon, which they could see from where they sat, was emptying. Men were putting on their hats and tying their scarves. Henry turned to Marcel, 'isn't it typical of the suburban scene,' he asked rhetorically, 'that it is an accumulation of trivialities? The novelties of this year are always being added to the novelties of last year, and these are always fading into insignificance until they are ready to emerge again in the character of the old and familiar things that we wondered at in childhood.' Marcel pondered the things that he had wondered at in childhood. What, after all, did they amount to?

II

Spring had come. The grounds of St Mary's Abbey at York were full of blossomed trees as Marcel and Henry went into the museum. An attendant told them where the meteorite was on display. They found it much smaller than they had expected. It had fallen, the inscription said, at 3.35 p.m. on Monday 14 March 1881 at Pennyman's siding on the Middlesbrough to Guisborough railway. It was recovered by three platelayers: Mr. Raw, Mr. Obren and Mr. Marley. A photograph showed them standing somewhat dazedly around the meteorite at the spot where it had fallen. 'So that's Jack Marley', exclaimed Marcel. He peered at the strong northern face and spare working class body. He was seeking for signs of profoundity, asceticism or atheleticism; he did not discover any. 'Henry,' he said, turning to the older, stouter man, 'you are trying to flee your own life. Mysticism is just as much a substitute for experience as is erudition'. 'If only we knew what Millie had looked like.' replied Henry, unmoved by Marcel's gratuitous and erroneous observation. Marcel, however, had moved off to examine a badly stuffed stoat which stared glassily at him from behind a shabby fern. He considered the limitations of Henry's powerful, subtle and immeasurable intelligence; it was still not the appropriate instrument for grasping the truth. What is most important to our hearts, he thought, shifting his gaze to a lugubrious but stoical badger whose coat was shiny where it was not bald, or to our minds is taught us not by reasoning but by other powers. To them intelligence must abdicate before it can become their collaborator and servant. He returned to Henry who was consulting his train time-table. There was a train for Dundee in two hours. They were on it when it drew out of York station.

They stayed at a hotel in the Blackness Road within easy reach of the Western Necropolis. As the train had moved out onto the bridge at Wormit Henry had expounded the tragedy of thirty-five

years before. Marcel had looked down on the broad
estuary, the evening light turning the water silver:
there was no menace in it. Geese flapped down river.
At Broughty Ferry a dreadnought lay at anchor; it
faced the bright sea swinging gently, its multi-
coloured bunting fluttering in the breeze. Marcel
had smiled at the brave sight. Later in the hotel
coming out of the lift and turning along the corridor
he had seen at its end an open window. The view was
towards the river and the hills of Fife beyond. On a
distant hill stood a single house, 'to which the
perspective and the evening light, while preserving
its mass, gave a gemlike precision and a velvet
casing, as though to one of those architectural works
in miniature, tiny temples or chapels wrought in
gold and enamel, which serve as reliquaries and are
exposed only on rare and solemn days for the veneration of the faithful' – so Marcel described it to
Henry at dinner – 'but this moment of adoration had
already lasted too long, for the maid came and drew
together, like those of a shrine, the two sides of the
window, and so shut off the minute edifice, the
glistening relic from my adoring gaze.' He tucked
his napkin into his collar and made a face at the
taste of his soup. He did not go on to tell Henry of his
discovery of the oratory-like servants' pantry at the
other end of the corridor, to which the maid had
returned after closing the window. The square panes
of crimson and yellow glass which framed the central, opaque panel of its only window had caught his
attention, for the evening sun cast upon the floor
such radiant, lozenged images of them that the maid
at the sink had been encircled with royal colours, in
her black and white uniform like the stigma of a
flower surrounded by its petals. Nor had his en-
chantment been broken by her smile, as hearing
him cough at last a little she had turned from her

washing of the dishes. Only her Dundee accent had
done that. Snapping out of his trance he had invited
her to his room; she was to come at eleven. Henry,
having pushed his unfinished soup aside, was talking. 'Is it just a girlish fad, feminine hysteria?' he
was asking. 'Why should it sweep the girls' schools
of Hampstead Garden Suburb and infect the novices
of two convents in the Fylde?' Marcel also surren-
dered in his contest with the soup and pushed his
plate to one side. The Galloway beef when it arrived
was much better. They ate ravenously. 'Isn't life,
collective life not individual lives, really a matter of
moods?, Marcel in his turn asked. 'When all is said
and done Henry, that is what history is. Look at us
now, what is the mood of us civilized, modern
Europeans? To put it no lower, aren't we in the mood
for a war. And won't they say of us, if there are any
left to say it, that we got our war because we were in
the mood for one?' Henry didn't answer. Such banal-
ity did not attract him. Why, he was thinking, do
they spoil this delicious beef by serving it with
swedes? The next morning they were on the Western
Necropolis. They found the grave with the help of
the cemetery's custodian: 'Domenico Antonio Iannetti. Died 12 March 1901. To our dear Dad.' From
the hilltop the Tay sparkled in the bright morning
light. The mudflats glistened. The geese were flying
inland. Dunsinane hill stood out sharply. 'Would
you have given your son the same name as yourself?', Marcel asked Henry. Henry made no answer.
Later that morning they hired a car and were driven
round by Perth to Balmerino. They walked about
the ivyied ruins of the abbey. From there Dundee's
grey buildings across the river were softened by
distance and the mid-day haze. If there had been a
relic had queen Ermengarde brought it here? Had
she brought the cult too? Had she danced here, an

English woman in Scotland remembering the giddy-
ness of her girlhood? It was so quiet among these
disordered stones Henry imagined he could hear the
faint sounds of shuffling, scuffing feet. Marcel,
however, believed even less in ghosts than he did in
History.

Kurt Schwitters was resolutely doing the breast-
stroke from end to end of the Public Baths at
Newcastle-under-Lyme when they arrived for their
swim. They had completed the ritual pilgrimage to
Penkhull. Adolescent girls had been swarming
everywhere, jostling and breathless. It was far more
to their taste in the Baths where only the splashing
of sedate afternoon swimmers broke the stillness.
After their swim Marcel took Henry and Kurt to The
Boat and Horses. As they sat comfortably in the
vaults Kurt showed them a doorknob with a blue
spot he had unscrewed from the door of his cubicle at
the Baths, and the pieces of lace curtain he had
snipped from the bottom of those at his lodging
house in Balliol Street. Later, this giant of
twentieth-century Art would use them and a cardboard box he had discovered under a table at a bar
near St Kunegunde's church in Cologne for one of
his *meisterwerke*, 'Picture with Spatial Growths-
Picture with Two Small Dogs'. Marcel and Henry
sipped their pints of bitter and made polite comments about Ruskin's views of the relation of Art to
Life, even if these lost something in the translation
the obliging and bilingual landlord had to make of
them for Kurt. He in turn endeavoured to tell them
of what they afterwards thought they had heard as
merz, so far as they could judge a word he used for
the image of the revolution within him not as it was
but as it should have been, and a prayer for the
victory peace would bring at the end of the next war,
in which Kurt informed them he would preserve

51

himself for the Fatherland and the History of Art by bravery behind the lines. They applauded this determinedly bold resolution, but thought they would never have the strength of mind to pursue such a course if war should come. How is this young man able to escape the common mood, they asked each other as they talked of their day before going to bed that night in the North Stafford Hotel. And yet to reflect it, they observed to one another at breakfast the following morning. One thing they agreed on was that in their disintegrating world the only legitimate response for the individual was to become either a gangster or a saint. 'Or, I suppose', Henry added, 'a giant of twentieth-century Art'. 'Wasn't it the same in the seventh century though': Marcel was thinking aloud. 'Perhaps you could dance yourself out of trouble or whirl your way clear of it'. He helped himself to more devilled kidneys from the sideboard and poured Henry a third cup of coffee. 'But then, couldn't you be gangster first and a saint afterwards, like St Guthlac?', said Henry, unimpressed by Marcel's insight. Marcel, however, was thinking neither very hard nor very deeply about either seventh-century sanctity or devilled kidneys. He was reflecting on that level ray of the setting sun, which, striking the wooden top of the bar in the vaults of The Boat and Horses as they had sat with Kurt the previous evening, had instantaneously transported him across time and space to Eulalie's little room, where as a child for a week he had been made to sleep because his aunt Léonie had been thought to have typhoid. Could art, could a life, true art, a true life, be fashioned from such fragments of refound time, given freely, not in answer to prayer or as reward for meritorious thought, but as of grace, -miracles of analogies? The miraculous which one could not go in search of, a kind of sanctity which

might not be cultivated, if any might? Were the
level ray of sun, the spoon against the plate, the
starched napkin, the noisy waterpipe, his *merz-
zeite*? He wished he could speak to Henry of these
things, but he could not bring himself to. How, after
all, had Henry reintegrated the disintegrating? By
sleight of language? More than that, much more
than that. Hadn't he understood that things were far
more complicated than people believed, and above
all grasped that complexity as well as the symmetry
which accompanies it was an element of beauty?
Henry's voice recalled him to his cooling kidneys
and their need to prepare to depart for London. 'If
there's an answer to that riddle I bet the great little
Rudyard will know it', was what he was saying.

III

It was not until August that they managed to meet
Kipling. They were staying with the Buxtons at
Castle House, Chipping Ongar when his letter from
Kessingland arrived. In the summer house on the
castle mound, with the ducks quacking around them
on the pelucidly green water below and the donkey
in his paddock braying like a badly tuned internal
combustion engine, Henry read it out to Marcel. It
was a perfect afternoon of undisturbed heat; Henry
in his broadbrimmed straw hat declaimed the letter
to a musing and amused Marcel, who had on his
boater with the Prussian blue band. 'My dear Henry,
isn't this it?', Henry read out,

> '"And David and all the house of Israel played before
> the Lord on all manner of instruments, on harps, on
> psalteries, on timbrels, on cornets and on cymbals. And
> David danced before the Lord with all his might and
> David was girded with a linen ephod. Michal, Saul's

daughter, looked through a window and saw king David leaping and dancing before the Lord. And Michal, the daughter of Saul, came out to meet David and said How glorious was the King of Israel today, who uncovered himself today in the eyes of the hand-maids of his servants as one of the vain fellows shamelessly uncovereth himself. And David said It was before the Lord which chose me, therefore will I dance before the Lord."

I will see you and your friend at Laxfield Low House today at five, ever your affectionate admirer, Rudyard.' Henry fanned himself with the large, heavy sheet of notepaper and looked at Marcel. His smile was broad. 'Of course, he's got it. Trust him. Where else but the Old Testament for an Anglo-Saxon? David in ecstasy before the Ark. Think of it Marcel, the impact of such imagery on the unsoph-isticated mind. And doesn't it confirm what we thought, doesn't it "wrap everything up" as the bishop said to the shop-girl?' Marcel winced at his companion's uncharacteristic lapse of taste. He ascribed it to Henry's bubbling excitement; the solving of an intellectual and artistic conundrum of such dimensions gave one the right to forget oneself for a moment, he considered forgivingly. He watched the handsome young manservant untie the boat below, stow their lemonade and macaroons carefully aboard, take up the oars and row across and around the moat. The drops of water rose and fell gleaming. He thought of Monet, of Bonnard, of Elstir. Of what each might have made of the young man's move-ments, the ripple at the boat's prow, the sparkling drops of water, the quivering, palpable afternoon air. Didn't they work with fragments too, the bits and pieces of a moment's impression? The lemonade was delicious: green in a green jug. He bit into his macaroon.

They drove to Laxfield through a green and gold landscape. Everywhere fields were full of harvesters. Dust and sweat flew. Horses stood patiently between the shafts of loaded wagons. Reapers paused to watch them slow down to pass. The stooping women staightened, their hands shading their eyes. Children ran about. In one empty, stubbled field an old woman was gleaning. In another the stooks marched off down a dip to a stream. Under deep hedgerows and tall trees baskets and bottles were scattered. Henry said: 'Can't you already smell the bread baking and the beer brewing?' Marcel sensed how this active, peopled landscape delighted Henry. Did it satisfy or appease his social conscience? They passed the Gothick lodges at the entrance to a great house, far out of sight down a drive which was being weeded by a score of gardeners picking their way on hands and knees, as if they were detectives searching for the conclusive clue to a hideous crime. 'You know what Rupert told me once', Henry said, as they turned round a corner and the fantastical lodges were lost to sight, 'he said it wasn't true that anger against injustice and wickedness and tyrannies was a good state of mind or noble, but with him as with most it was a dirty, mean and choky emotion. He *hates* the upper classes.' Marcel, by way of reply or of avoiding a reply, recited the forty-ninth psalm, 'a rich man without understanding is like the beasts that perish.' 'This is a biblical day', laughed Henry, 'I shouldn't be surprised to find Ruth and Boaz around the next bend. Instead, it was the mighty tower of Laxfield church. They left the car at the gate and walked down to the Low House. Kipling was seated outside. Inside, when Marcel went to buy their pints of bitter from a plumpish women who reminded him at once of the landlady of the Potwell Inn, he found no other customers. 'Too early yet for folk to be in from the fields', she said, drawing the beer from the barrel in her neat kitchen. He returned to find Henry explaining to Kipling Iannetti's connection with the fourteenth-century manuscript of Jalal al-Din Rumi's Discourses and how at Venice Miss Tita had once shown him the unforgettable illumination on the verso of the fifth folio. Marcel drank his golden beer meditatively; he saw that Kipling was not only not impressed but also thoroughly unconvinced. He wanted to talk about the war. He had soon punctured Henry's effervescent mood, though not, as Marcel could see, his belief in their discovery. Yet Marcel saw with equal clarity that just as Kipling's irrepressible, unstoppable flow of war talk was reducing Henry to a subdued, even a mortified silence, which patently he found discomforting, so would the war itself obscure, perhaps obliterate that extraordinary discovery. Marcel knew him well enough to discern that Henry knew it too, that he understood, as Kipling talked purposefully and intelligently on and on, that their historical detection would never receive the recognition it deserved. They had been overtaken by Armageddon, upstaged by the Apocalypse. Their eyes met over Kipling's head. Marcel did his best to make his express his sympathy and understanding. He turned away. Henry went for more beer. Kipling went to the lavatory. Marcel stared at the shadows the churchyard elms were throwing on the yellow-washed gable end of a cottage up the hill. The clock in the church tower struck the half-hour. How was he to convert these sensations into their spiritual equivalents? By thought surely, but by what type of thinking? Like Henry's, but unlike. Kipling came back and abruptly interrupted him. Had he been to Swaffham Bulbec yet, he asked. 'Its from your Balbec', he added, knocking out his pipe against the arm of the bench they were sitting on and reaching for the glass Henry was offering him.

IV

Early October found them at Hampton Court: they stood in the viewing gallery of the Royal Tennis Court. Erskine Childers was playing Charles Fryatt; it would be these two heroes' last match. Henry and Marcel watched Childers heavily under-cut his service onto the Grille penthouse via the Side penthouse; the ball descended with barely any momentum, but it was perfectly struck by Fryatt into the Dedans. The players changed ends nodding agreeably to Marcel and Henry. Fryatt now served; Childers returned the ball hard and high; it ricochetted off the wall above the Side penthouse onto the back wall before falling sharply to the floor of the court. Fryatt hit it firmly to the Tambour, off which it flew at right angles to the Side penthouse roof from where it rolled rather than bounced onto the floor at the very rear of the Hazard side. Childers could not reach it in time. Fryatt claimed his point. 'They have no marker', exlaimed Marcel. Thorough-ly astonishing Henry, Marcel went into the Mar-ker's Box and signalled his intention to the players. Henry moved into the Dedans and sat down. Per-plexed but absorbed he observed the match and listened to Marcel's calling and marking of the Chases with an admiration mixed with no little pride in this hitherto unrecorded and unexpected skill of his friend. Charles Fryatt's greater strength eventually decided the match in the tenth game of the third set: Childers was unable to reach a fierce return which plummetted obliquely and alarmingly into the Winning Gallery. Marcel received the enthusiastic thanks of the two players and then rejoined Henry. They walked out into the sunshine. 'I always thought you were fooling in that photograph', Henry remarked as having traversed the length of the East Front of the palace they left the Broad Walk and entered the Privy Garden. Here Marcel pulled out his watch. 'We have twenty minutes yet', he said, replacing it. They sat on iron chairs. It was a warm Saturday afternoon and the visitors paused frequently in their strolling to appreciate the michaelmas daisies and autumn crocuses. There were innumerable babies in perambulators being pushed conscientiously by their blue or brown uniformed nannies. There were also many men in khaki. Henry sighed. 'Did you see in *The Times* this morning that John Currie killed his Dolly and then himself?' Marcel nodded. 'Did you see what he had written?', he went on, pulling a newspaper cutting out of his pocketbook and reading from it, '"I still love her but her worthlessness makes life impossible. I would gladly go to the war but this has unfitted me for a soldier."' Marcel did not answer; with his cane he made patterns in the white gravel between his feet. Henry returned the cutting to his pocketbook and the pocketbook to his pocket and began to duplicate Marcel's patterns in the gravel with his walking stick. 'I suppose you wouldn't believe all that we do is wholly subjective, would you Henry', Marcel finally asked breaking into their quietness, 'a pursuit of the projections of our own mind?'. 'No', replied Henry, but I do believe you and I are like St. Paul, imposters who speak the truth. Come, we must go to see if Iannetti is in the Orangery. He hasn't come this way or he would have passed us.' When they entered the cool room he was already there. Marcel stopped at the doorway. 'Ah, if only they would hang the Mantegna cartoons in here', he exclaimed. Henry crossed to where Iannetti was standing by the windows, looking out to Wren's Banqueting House beyond the Sunk Garden. Marcel went after him. 'Will he have it?', he whispered. Henry did not respond. He was intent on the piece of paper Iannetti had slipped into his hand. On it in Arabic was a name which he knew should be the final link in a chain binding two civilizations together, the most exotic and most exciting example of cultural diffusion he or Marcel had ever come across. They pored uncomprehendingly over the slip of paper. 'And how do you say it?', demanded Henry of the young man who was eager to be gone. Iannetti bent closer, and as they craned their heads in concentration spoke distinctly the name they were longing to hear. 'Binkit', he said and hesitated at their consternation, 'there is no P in Arabic'.

For Francois Truffaut 1984

5

The Downham Tablet

recto

O sanctae saltatrices Penket et Pega,
orate pro nobis in hoc plano mariscosoque
purgatorio; o virgines pudicissime,
transmutate nos aquosos in celorum
vinum; dolorosos ad karkarandum
convertite; o sorores hagagares, orate pro
nobis Edwardo et Ricardo et pro anima Anne.

verso

the eve of seynt sixburghe. trust thys fysychon.
we are kepyt streygth nowe. oure lyves are worthles.
yn the name off Jesu.

THE DOWNHAM TABLET was discovered in 1721 by
villagers digging for peat in Church Fen, Little
Downham, an unpretentious village in the Isle of
Ely. Its discovery was immediately communicated to
Maurice Johnson, renowned antiquarian founder
and secretary of the Spalding Gentlemen's Society.
It was barely damaged, only suffering the merest
knick to its upper edge by a peat cutter's hodding or
paring spade, for it was discovered just below, in-

deed embedded in, the top layer of earth before the peat is reached. It was also entirely legible, which so far as its recto side is concerned, was almost miraculous. Some unknown chemical interaction between the ink and Church Fen water must have taken place to work as a preservative, so far as I am aware, a unique instance of this, as invariably in waterlogged conditions ink is washed off. The tablet was of beech wood, three quarters of an inch thick, eight inches wide by six inches deep. Soil conditions, as in Novgorod and at Vindolanda, were ideal in the fen for the preservation of an object of organic material.

At the roman fort of Vindolanda in Northumberland some ninety writing tablets mainly of limewood have been found since 1973. The writing on them in a carbon-based ink has been read by photographing it with infra-red film. Some of these tablets are letters home asking for woollen socks and underpants, one is a letter of recommendation, timeless in its language of solicitation, another is one of a series evidently deriving from the quartermaster: it states the issue from stores of beer, wine, pork and barley. At Novgorod the tablets are of birch bark; the writing has been scratched on. More than four hundred from the Middle Ages have been discovered. They range over a wide variety of subjects. My favourite is the one whose abridged beginning is all that survives: 'From Nikita to Ulyanitsa. Marry me. I want you and you me. And as witness will be Ignato . . .' Presumably the tough task of scratching on the words was an aid to brevity, as we can detect in the verso of the Downham Tablet where also the message was scratched into the wood. One Novgorod tablet has the letters of the Russian alphabet upon it. It was undoubtedly used for teaching and was fixed to the wall, as can be seen from the holes drilled in it. From Maurice Johnson's description of the Downham Tablet, with its four holes at the corners, it too had once been fixed to the wall.

We have to rely on Johnson's description and also his transcription (which stands at the head of this paper) because the tablet itself did not survive into the age of modern historical scholarship, let alone into that of sophisticated archaeological techniques. It was burnt in the kitchen stove of the premises of the Spalding Gentlemen's Society during their renovation in the winter of 1792 by a caretaker who was not merely cold; he was later suspected of having Jacobin sympathies and, perhaps not inappropriately as it will appear in the sequel, antiroyalist leanings. Unfortunately and much to my regret the tablet cannot be submitted to those rigorous tests which these days immediately determine the authenticity or otherwise of unusual material from the past.

All this is dry, historical fact, but I can assure you, essential to establish the context of what will follow. There is, however, human interest. Here I am, age twelve I think, my eye already firmly fixed on the mystery of the Downham Tablet. It is Brighton beach but my mind is in the fens of East Anglia. The book open before me contains a modern account of Maurice Johnson's report to the Spalding Gentlemen's Society of the finding of the tablet and his attempt at its elucidation. I was enthralled, but even at that tender and usually credulous age, I was not convinced by his ideas about its origin and function. There, then, my obsession began: on Brighton beach, *circa* 1947. Here I am also, writing this time. It is in the sunny garden of the meeting house of the Spalding Gentlemen's Society in the summer of 1963. On holiday, I have taken the opportunity of paying my first visit to Maurice Johnson's own immense manuscript collection kept there in the

Society's library. I am transcribing Johnson's notes, which have formed the basis of almost all my subsequent inquiries. Why was I obsessed, you may be asking yourselves. So far, my answer to that question, one which you will realize I have often put to myself, is that there are also mysteries where historical enquiry and endeavour are found. Probably, I have to admit, my obsession was neither as deep nor as consistent as I would like you to believe. Other interests intervened, even sometimes jostled the obsession to one side for a spell: marriage, children, religion, Stoke City Football Club, for instance. Yet I had a firm feeling that Johnson's fourteenth-century dating, arrived at before palaeography and diplomatic had become systematic disciplines, was incorrect.

Maurice Johnson had not identified Penket. Pega, being fairly local, he had: she was the sister of St Guthlac and Spalding is less than fifteen miles from Peakirk. For want of any evidence to the contrary he had described Penket as another sister of Guthlac and left it at that. Nor, being a poor Hebraist, had he got very far with the latter part of the tablet. He had toyed with the idea of the two saintly sisters as tumblers, but eventually, though confessing his bemusement, he correctly construed 'saltatrices' as dancers. After all, the erudite of eighteenth-century England must have been as distant from appreciating the sacramental quality of ecstatic dance as the educated of any age or culture ever have been.

Yet ecstatic dancing, unlikely attribute as it might seem to be of seventh-century Anglo Saxon saints, is what Penket and Pega were honoured for, and not only by those for whom, I believe, the tablet was made. Unlikely? It is not when we remember that Penket was Irish. I have indicated elsewhere the grounds for the case that Penket was one of the few dancing or whirling saints in Western Christendom. Pega presents some difficulties, but I suppose she has to be accounted another, even if she was not revered by Muslims as Penket was and is, specifically by the Mehlevis, or sect of the Whirling Dervishes as they are more usually called in the West. It was in a manuscript of the Discourses of Jalal al-Din Rumi, the Mehlevis' thirteenth-century founder, that I came across the first identifiable picture of St Penket. It is revealing and ironic that she, a Christian saint, found her true disciples in another culture, another religion.

By many devious ways and lucky chances I was led from my knowledge of Penket as ecstatic dancer to the Millie Marley Sect. I have said that Penket had no true disciples in the West; that was certainly not the case in the last twenty years of the nineteenth century when the Millie Marley Sect came into being through an extraordinary sequence of misconceptions about a series of events which included the plummeting to earth of the Middlesbrough meteorite and a phenomenally low tide on the Tees at the village of Yarm in Yorkshire. Still, I do not consider the Millie Marleyians as true followers of St Penket, honour her as they do in their own way. In their formative days they fell under the spell of the *Gnostic Acts of John*, and took as their watch-word the line from its eucharistic hymn 'Who so dances not, knows not what comes to pass'. To whatever lengths one may go in accepting dance as prayer, and I for one will go a fair distance, such a singleminded exclusiveness will not do at all. Sometimes, nonetheless, the devil has to be supped with; one has simply to make sure the cutlery is the right kind. What I did, I had to do to advance my knowledge of Penket and of the tablet, for there was every hope that my pursuit of the former would bring me nearer an understanding of the latter. A former student put me in touch with a young couple in Strood, Kent, who were members of a Millie Marley group which she said, met periodically at Hoo, one of the most out of the way places in south eastern England. The couple, as you might expect, refused to talk at all at first, but were given away by their young daughter who spontaneously performed what I knew to be an untaxing training dance for novices. They would not tell me a great deal, but they did give me the names of two of the national co-ordinators of the sect. These two young women – for men are only tolerated, not welcomed by Millie Marleyians – agreed to meet me at a secluded inn deep in the Forest of Dean.

They, under my determined questioning, gave me what I thought I needed for my enquiries to be taken a stage further: they disclosed the Jewish influence on the Sect's dancing rituals, an influence I had suspected, as anyone having come to know the Millie Marleyians' reverence for the Old Testament would have suspected, and they revealed the whereabouts of an heretical group for whom they exhibited a vitriolic disdain but who they thought might know of the whereabouts of those Hasidic Jews who could tell me more of Penket and the ecstatic dance. Thus, I came to Crewe. Of all places, it was one I thought I knew well; I had never imagined I would find there such an eccentric off-shoot of the Millie Marley Sect as the Crew Cygnets.

Under the pretence of being a formation swimming club these athletic and after their fashion devout young women performed the water dances which had led to their expulsion from the mainstream Millie Marleyians. At Crewe Swimming Baths, a relic of the taste of the 1930s, I watched the skilful and aesthetic interweaving of the ring dance,

here transformed for it was swum in and under the
water. Performing as they had to in public, their
peculiar aquatic rites constraining them to do so, the
ecstatic content of their dance appeared muted.
When I met the leader of the group afterwards in her
costume of the 1930s, for like the Old Amish and the
Hutterian Brethren the Crewe Cygnets are committed to the dress and behaviour of the epoch of their
beginning she seemed pleased by my interest in
what she called her and her colleagues' life work and
was surprisingly frank in her answers to my questions. It was strange to be drinking a cup of tea in
Flag Lane, Crewe at the very heart of the English
Midlands and to be listening to her speak such an
exotic litany of names, the names of Prague, Cracow, Zamość, Mukachevo, Jerusalem, Zafed, Cana in
Galilee. In one of those places, she told me, I would
find him, that *zaddik* who knew and cherished the
history of Jewish dance and its influence upon
religious dance in the Christian West. He will not be
easy to find, she flung after me, as I boarded my bus.
Nor was he the following summer during what
turned out to be for me an itinerant holiday.

I began in Prague at the old synagogue. Told there
of his hotel I was just too late to catch him. In
Cracow I arrived seconds after he and a friend had
been enjoying a beer together. At Zamość I glimpsed
him in the town library, but by the time I had found
my way back to the entrance hall it was closing time
and I was the last to be let out by the punctual
custodian. In Mukachevo I sat in the Talmudic
school waiting for his anticipated coming. Did he
come? If so I missed him or no one bothered to tell
me he had arrived, or sitting down to eat they all
forgot I needed to be told. So it had to be Jerusalem;
at the Western Wall I saw him, only to lose him
again as I was overwhelmed by the midmorning

onslaught of Brooklyn families bringing their boys
to make Bar Mitzvah. On then to Zafed, where from
the balcony of my hotel on an otherwise motionless
shabbat I looked down on him dancing along to
Simon Luria's synagogue. I caught up with him
there, but not daring to interrupt I was told to go to
his home in Cana where he would be the next day.
So it was in Cana of Galilee where our Lord worked
such a homely miracle and which so vividly reminded me of the Downham Tablet, that rabbi Levin
gave me the information which carried me to the
crucial, penultimate phase of my enquiries.

Firstly, during those long discussions into the hot
August nights, while outside in the narrow street
boys played marbles in the light from the open door
and nuns went to and fro, rabbi Levin spoke of the
eleven Hebrew verb roots to describe dancing; there
had been among the Jews he said an advanced stage
of choreography. Two of those verbs made sense to
me at once: the most famous of them, used also to
mean a festival, *hagag*, to dance in a circle, and the
most intriguing of them, *karkar*, to rotate with all
one's might, as David did before the Ark. David also,
it may be added, jumped, skipped and danced around
it in a circle. My heart jumped too, and I nearly got
up and danced in a circle for here was what Penket
and Pega were up to in the tablet. But who in
medieval England had the Hebrew to describe them
so accurately as whirling and circling? 'Then shall
the Virgin rejoice in the dance', rabbi Levin was
murmuring, his eyes twinkling in the lamplight.
'The dances of the Jew before his creator are
prayers', I said softly in response, wondering as I
said those famous words whether Penket and Pega
thought of their dancing in that way. Clearly that, it
now seemed to me, was the point of it.

Secondly, and more startingly, rabbi Levin told

me of the Florentine Jews, of Miriam and of the
Medici. Much has been written recently of the urban
youth culture of the Renaissance, particularly of the
dance and drama confraternities which were an
attempt to keep Florentine young men off the
streets, or rather to put them there only on certain
occasions under, so to speak, controlled conditions.
While their fathers were whipping themselves and
then sitting down to a good meal every other Tuesday, their sons were having to sing, act and dance
under the watchful eyes of Observant Friars. Dancing in fact was so much a part of fashionable life in
fifteenth-century Florence that one distinguished
art historian has described Botticelli's style as
'dancerly', a style created expressly for businessmen
whose relaxation after a hard day at the office
making two and two five, if it was not flagellation
night, was to dance. A little of this I outlined to
rabbi Levin; of course, he replied, it was all the
result of the Jews and Miriam. Apparently, interest
in Torah and Kabala had for a brief time among
Jewish intellectuals in early fifteenth-century Florence focused on Aaron's sister. It had to do with
gematria. As rabbi Levin's deep East European voice
wove rich patterns of words and numbers I, lulled
almost into a doze, caught only the interconnected-
ness of Miriam's circular dance, the patronage of
Cosimo de Medici, the Florentine vision of heaven,
and the Messianic strand in Pico della Mirandola's
thinking and Sandro Botticelli's painting.

What brought me out of my trance at Cana that
particular night was a name rabbi Levin dropped
into his discourse, an unmistakable name, though
he pronounced it in its Arabic form, *Binkit*. Two
names actually, for in his next sentence he was
linking with St Penket a person who at once brought
me back if not to Downham then to Ely, a person

who enabled me for the first time to put a date to the tablet. That person, as rabbi Levin pronounced the name, oddly enough in what was its medieval form, was Tiptot, that is John Tiptoft, earl of Worcester, whose tomb is in the cathedral. Their connection was straightforward. All the intellectual talk in Florence in the 1450s while Tiptoft had been in Italy trying to steer clear of involvement in complicated English politics was of that dancing British saint. When Tiptoft came to Florence in 1461, thoroughly at home in Italian and entirely captivated by Italian *mores*, he was undoubtedly informed, probably by Giovanni Medici with whom he stayed at Fiesole, of the cult of his compatriot: Penket was all the rage. She had been a virtuous dancer and she was not Jewish. Those Christian businessmen had found a saint to suit their taste. Their Jewish friends had introduced them to her, for in the Talmudic schools of Florence there had been much weighing of the numerical values of the names of Miriam and Penket, a Penket well known to Florentine Jews from their contacts with Sufis of the Levant. The devotion to Penket, as with so much else in Renaissance Florence, was a passing fancy, a fad almost; it was on the wane by 1462, had disappeared by 1463. Yet so fashionable had she been, even Fra Angelico, I believe, had been prevailed upon to paint her just before his death in 1455 as one of the saints in heaven. Moreover, this was in the predella of the altar-piece for the church of the Dominican house near Fiesole of which he himself was prior. If I am right, and you can check for yourselves by going to the National Gallery to see what the late Director, Sir Martin Davies, called 'by far the most distinguished hagiological picture in the Gallery', then this is the second representation of St Penket which has come to light. The third was quickly to follow.

Let me summarize what I had learnt in Cana: the
tablet was composed by someone thoroughly at
home in the Hebrew vocabulary of the dance; there
had been a cult of St Penket in upper class circles in
Florence when Tiptoft had visited that city in 1461.
Tiptoft I knew had Cambridgeshire connections;
these fens were also part of his world. But the names
on the tablet did not fit anyone associated with
Tiptoft during his life, a life which had been cut
short in 1470; nor was there a shred of evidence that
he knew any Hebrew. Tiptoft seemed somehow a
link; he was not the answer. In addition, I needed,
despite all the trust I had in rabbi Levin, conclusive
proof of Tiptoft's knowledge of Penket. If he was to
be a link I had to make him a secure one. I was
shortly to find that proof and very much else which
was germane. More quickly than I could ever have
hoped or wished for I was to return to Downham via
Wiggenhall St Mary Magdalene and Bridgnorth.

Once I had Tiptoft's name one thing followed
another fairly logically, as the literary and
documentary sources for his life and interests have
been exhaustively examined. This is not, however,
the case so far as the saints associated with him in
the stained glass of the north aisle of Wiggenhall St
Mary Magdalene church, Norfolk, are concerned.
Those were, as you may imagine, my first thought.
Sure enough St Penket is, or I think she is, there,
the third representation of her which we have to
date. The glass at Wiggenhall was almost certainly
the gift in her uncle's memory of Joan Ingold-
sthorpe, Tiptoft's niece. She, like her mother Joan,
who put up the memorial to him where his head and
body were buried at the Black Friars in London and
who probably paid for his tomb in Ely cathedral,
seems to have remembered Tiptoft with gratitude,
probably with affection. The saints Isobel chose for

71

him at Wiggenhall deserve detailed study; his taste, fastidious in such matters, might then be better known and understood. Among them are Italians: St Prosdocimus of Padua, St Januarius of Naples, St Hippolytus, and St Brizio or Brice, apostle of Umbria. There are also the British: Samson, Aldhelm, Cuthbert, perhaps Alban. I say perhaps, because not all the saints can be identified from the incomplete inscriptions which survive, but there can be no doubt about Penket even if the 'et' is missing. Thus, one matter was cleared up. Yet, what of the Hebrew of the tablet, its author, date and place? The answers to these questions came almost all at once and at Bridgnorth. It was a straightforward task to consult the *Liber Epistolarum* of Tiptoft in Lincoln Cathedral Library; more complicated was eating a meal in that beautiful city, or at least consuming it while resisting the advances of the waiter who attempted some remarkable passes with a red paper napkin. The Cathedral Library was a quieter, cooler place altogether; seated unmolested, I found in the Letter Book John's extravagantly and warmly expressed request to John Argentine, a Cambridge graduate in Florence, to bring back with him when he returned to England a copy of Lucretius' *de Rerum Natura*, parenthetically a volume, whose title at any rate, that waiter might have been advised to study. This letter was the breakthrough. Here was the name of another man with Italian experience and interests, a man who connected so perfectly with the christian names of the tablet, that I knew I was almost home.

Triumphantly, therefore, I went to Bridgnorth. I knew what I was going to see and what I would find. The famous Claverley Manuscript had been accurately described when it had been deposited in Bridgnorth Public Library around the turn of this century. Going to view it was made a special pleasure by the ascent to the library on the Cliff cable railway, one of the delights of a delightful town. The Claverley Manuscript, so called because it had been in the Claverley church chest since John Argentine's death in 1508, is an ecclectic collection of short pieces or tracts, two of them printed. Most of these are medical, three of them are astrological, one is on geomancy, the one I was after is in Hebrew. It concerns drugs and their concoction, and purports to be written by a Doctor Moses Kohen of Florence. It had notes by Argentine in English (including his recipe for a potion: take wild plums crushed with strong ale, 'And drynke thereof most in tyme of peyne'), in poor Italian and, what I had come for, even poorer Hebrew. Yet Hebrew it was. John Argentine, therefore, knew enough Hebrew to write it. There was nothing about dancing; that would have been too much to expect.

I had, then, a man who had been friendly with Tiptoft, a man who either through Tiptoft or through his own Italian experience, would have been aware of the cult of the dancing Penket, a man who understood Hebrew and was able to write it. Also, a man who had the opportunity to write it for Edward and Richard: he was, after all, their doctor. In 1478 Dr John Argentine entered the royal service. In 1483, by his own testimony to an Italian visitor to London, he had been one of the last to see his two most distinguished patients alive. I may say that he must have one of the most dismally unsuccessful records of all time for a doctor, and here I am about to reveal the identity of the two boys for whom the Downham Tablet was composed: Dr Argentine lost his foremost patient in April 1483 when King Edward IV suddenly collapsed and died, cause undiagnosed, he lost two others in July 1483, our Edward and Richard, who when Argentine said goodbye to them in the Tower looked, on his own admission, pretty peaky and who were shortly to disappear altogether, and, if that was not failure enough, Prince Arthur, eldest son of King Henry VII, died on him in 1502. None of this prevented John Argentine, a Bottisham boy, from becoming Provost of King's College, Cambridge – not an unsuitable reward, one might think, for such undistinguished service. With such a record, one wonders whether he was not also attending Anne Mowbray, the last of the Mowbrays, when she slipped away not yet aged nine in November 1481. It is undoubtedly Anne's soul for which Penket and Pega are urged to dance and pray in the tablet: she had been the wife of Prince Richard, duke of York, aged four when they were married in January 1478.

When was the tablet composed? Where did it hang? And what of the scratched message of the verso? Here I am in the realm of conjecture, informed and resonable though it may be. The tablet, it appears to me, had to have been written between the death of Anne on 21 November 1481 and the eve of St Sexburgha, that is 5 July, of that year which may truthfully be termed traumatic, 1483. Moreover, it seems to have been composed while the princes were on a visit to the fens: perhaps they had been unhappily to Cambridge with their doctor. The tablet probably hung in Edward, prince of Wales' oratory, possibly in the royal chapel, though I suspect the latter would have been far too public a place for it. Did the two boys dance? Did Argentine encourage them? Was ecstatic whirling good for adolescents? Did they take wild plums crushed in strong ale after their exertions? Was that why they looked so pale on the eve of their Uncle Richard's coronation, which was duly held on St Sexburgha's feast day, 6 July 1483? Had they been overdoing their devotions as death closed in on them? But my fancy is beginning to take wing. The verso, nonetheless, does show that the princes knew their end was very near. As John Argentine carried away the tablet from the Tower he knew it too. Did he deliver the message on its verso? I am sure he did.

Here, at last we are back at Downham. The final exclamation of the verso gives the game away so far as its intended recipient is concerned. The governor of his household is the man Edward, prince of Wales is likely to have written to. That man was also the founder of Jesus college, Cambridge; evidently he and his young charge shared an interest in the new devotion to the Name of Jesus. John Alcock, therefore, was the man who received the princes' resigned but informative last words. When he became bishop of Ely in 1486 and began at once to rebuild the episcopal palace at Little Downham he brought to it a relic of the recent murderous past. No doubt he treasured it. Other, later bishops did not; one day it was thrown out as unwanted lumber. Recovered in 1721 it perished for good in 1792. Fortunately for us, however, Maurice Johnson's timely transcription has been enough for a reconstruction of the tablet's genesis and early history. Now, perhaps, I can shed my obsession with the Downham Tablet and, if it is not too late, get down to some real history.

A slightly extended and illustrated version of this paper was read at the Deanery, Ely, on 2 August 1985.

6

Kurt Schwitters in England

MARCEL PROUST left Paris on Thursday 2 October 1902. He arrived in Bruges the same day and immediately visited the hospital of St. John to see the Memlings. 'The Mystic Marriage of S. Catherine' (he wrote in an unpublished letter to his friend Prince Antoine Bibesco) 'is a pageant of colours, no a riot, a rising, a rebellion of the colours: they spring out upon you. Of Memling I must see more and, my dear Antoine, I shall, for tomorrow I take ship to England. Am I mad you ask? (I can see those creases about your eyes forming as you read on). The Channel in October, Marcel adrift and asthmatic in the mist. Ah but I have to go, to see what they all say here is Memling's masterpiece. It is at Chatsworth where the Duke of Devonshire lives; you remember his niece last year, that September afternoon at the Café Weber? She was in lilac and pretended she hated Paris. Well, it is to Chatsworth I have to go to see the grandest of this grand Memling's works . . .' The letter continues but on other matters; it was dated from the Hotel Royale, Ostend, 11 p.m. 2 October. He did not however see his grandest of grand Memlings. Chatsworth was shut up; the ducal household was away in Scotland; and the housekeeper refused to admit this oddly dressed and pale young man without a card. He pleaded. She remained firm. He fled. He came, improbable as it may seem, to Stoke-on-Trent and there, at a loose end on the Saturday afternoon and already dreading the Sunday that was to follow, he left the North Stafford Hotel and wandering at random found himself at the open end of the Victoria Ground. He paid his money and went in; the match had already, though only just, begun. Proust was, according to his own admission, enthralled. 'The sun shone through the hazy afternoon sky as if through muslin. I shielded my eyes: figures in red and white and in black and white ran and came together, parted, jumped, fell, and ran again. They must have had a purpose but I certainly could not discern it. Their movements to me turned upon an unknowable discipline, some inner compulsion, which made of them ceaseless pursuers of a goal that was beyond me and perhaps – being in their imaginations only – beyond them too. But not' (he goes on in this unfortunately fragmentary passage which only very recently has been brought to light) 'beyond the dark-haired youth who stood beside me. He, his fingers inside his mouth, blew raucous whistles, apparently, though this was not easy to detect, of approbation for the heroes who careered about the field before us. He had large ears with flat heavy lobes, and . . .' (here the fragment ends). Proust, none the worse for his fleeting visit to England and the Potteries, was in Antwerp by 9 October. He was in his thirty-second year.

The black-haired, big-eared boy by whom he had spent the October afternoon watching Stoke City play Grimsby Town was in his sixteenth year. He was Kurt Schwitters. Over from Germany with his father, they had journeyed from Hanover the pre-

vious Wednesday and were due to return the following Tuesday. Kurt's father had come to discuss a
contract for the supply of potash to Messrs Durridge
and Joyce, chemists to the Pottery trade (and in
1902 the most respected firm in that line in the
Potteries). Kurt, supposedly accompanying his
father to learn the business, but in reality already
collecting those bits and pieces of other folks' rub-
bish with which to make his *Merzbilder*, Kurt too
was at a loose end that Saturday, and, seeing a
poster half hanging from a wall (part of which he at
once lovingly conveyed to the deep pocket of his long
jacket, his *Merzenthaltensammlung* as he affec-
tionately called it) he decided to go where it directed
him, the Victoria Ground. He tells (in a privately
printed and now rare pamphlet, published at
Weimar in 1934) how he spent most of the match
practising his whistling; knowing nothing of the
protagonists his whistling, though entirely for his
own pleasure and not directed against anyone in
particular was taken amiss by those among whom
he stood. 'Their taunts', writes Kurt, 'became
threats. I desisted. But a minute later I could not
resist a long blast at an elderly player in red and
white stripes, who despite his age was a firm
favourite of those around me. Their anger and my
single strident whistle made a man standing beside
me, who had not joined in the hostility of the others,
laugh. When he had stopped he lent towards me and
said these words, words which I have never forgotten and which now' – Kurt was writing, remember,
in Germany in 1934 – 'are more to be borne in mind
than ever, that unknown man said quietly yet quite
distinctly: "Don't let the bastards grind you down."'

In memoriam: 18 November 1976 – 8 January 1977

79

7

The Day Henry James
Discovered Dada

HANS ARP, present with his twelve children and with
a brioche in his left nostril, did not know the whole
story. It was not at the Café de la Terrasse, Zurich,
at six p.m. on 6 February 1916 that Dada was
invented, but at the ground of the Chislehurst
Cricket Club at three p.m. on 10 July 1872. I do not
want to contradict the generally accepted view that
it was in that cafe at that hour on that day that
Tristan Tzara 'first uttered the word'; far from it;
what I wish at last to disclose is where he got the
word from. For the discovery of Dada was no accident, no gratuitous act, no chance connection. That
pivotal moment, upon which the twentieth century
has ever since spun, despite the conspiracy Vladimir
Ilyich in the next street was hatching to stop its
spinning dead, was long in preparation. So why then
Dada, at six p.m. on the sixth? If the answer is not to
be found in an explosion of unreason surfacing from
the unconscious like Moby Dick from the depths,
where is it to be found? It is in fact found in the
London *Times* of 2 February which on 6 February
had (by train through wartime France) just reached

Zurich. On coming into the cafe at five p.m. Tzara hooked it down from *der zeitungsspanner* with his walking stick and carried it across to his usual table. In it on page eleven he found Dada. At six p.m., his friends having gathered about him, he spoke the word and the twentieth century burst into being.

What was Dada doing on page eleven of *The Times* of 2 February 1916? Amid items concerning Zeppelin bomb damage in Staffordshire, the accidental death of Sir Clements Markham, 'fatally burnt while reading in bed by the light of a candle which he had been holding in his hand' in his electrically-lit bedroom, and the use of knives in the trenches ('this throttling is an unpractical makeshift'), it appeared under the heading 'condition of invalids' and between reports on the Earl of Essex (he had had a better night) and the Bishop of Gloucester (he was in bed with an attack of neuritis) in a quite lengthy account of Henry James' last illness. For some weeks, since a series of strokes, James had been wandering in his mind. 'One name', the piece reads, 'predominates in our great novelist's sad ramblings, a name to which over and over he returns: Napoleon ... And, almost as often, he remembers his father, continually repeating Dada, Dada, Dada.' The feeble analysis then proferred in the article that Bonaparte and James' father had somehow become associated in James' failing mind is, as we might expect, erroneous (as well as feeble). Henry James was remembering not the first Napoleon but the third, and not his dear old dad but an exclamation made by an excited child on the same memorable occasion of his encounter with the Emperor. That of course had been at three p.m. on 10 July 1872 at the ground of the Chislehurst Cricket Club.

Henry, touring in Europe that summer and briefly over in London, had accepted an invitation to play for the Downing College Daisies, a scratch eleven, captained that year by another writer of style and sensibility, F.W. Maitland, fresh from triumph in the Cambridge Moral Science Tripos. By 10 July they were near the end of their tour of Kent, and short of a man (who earlier than anticipated had had to join his family's yacht bound for the Mediterranean) one of the team said he would get Henry down for the day to Chislehurst: 'he'd love a game, you know what these American fellers are once they take to something.' So, delighted to escape 'the grimness of London', down Henry came. Out in the afternoon sun, deep at long on in front of the windmill where the bracken of the common came up to the boundary of the playing field, and spruce if not agile, he shielded his eyes against the sun, and when need be (which mercifully was not often) he ran after the ball. Alas, just before three p.m. Henry saw 'with an apparently inhibiting trepidation' the batsman swing mightily into a short-pitched ball, which soared into the sun and flew with a flawless accuracy towards long on. 'The Sun, the ball, and my heart suddenly stopped. Then, after a timeless pause, and just as suddenly, they all started again: my heart beat, the sun moved, and the ball sped into my upthrust hands. I stumbled, fell, and rolled over. When I opened my eyes it was to see the amazed faces of my teammates, who clustering around me, stretched upon the ground, were staring at the ball which (God knows how) I still clasped. Then they and the spectators broke into cheering; their shouts of bravo even more than the tightness with which I continued to grip the ball confirmed for me that the miraculous had happened.'

Stunned, and sore from the slaps on the back of his

delighted colleagues, Henry related how his feeling
of 'other-worldliness' was intensified when a smartly
turned-out manservant appeared beside him, lifted
his hat and said: 'The Emperor, sir, offers his con-
gratulations on your remarkable feat and requests
that you do it again.' Henry had not noticed the
arrival of Napoleon III and the Empress Eugénie in
their carriage; now as he got to his feet he saw them
on the far side of the ground towards Camden Place,
sitting stiff and upright, he smoking a cigarette and
still applauding, she under her magenta parasol
applauding too. As he looked towards them they
inclined their heads in recognition. It was at this
precise moment that two things happened: the sun
catching the harness of the horse as it suddenly
shifted, snorting at the hullabaloo, flashed a shaft of
reflected light across the field to dazzle the already
bewitched long on, and, as his eyes were so magical-
ly assailed, so were his ears, for from behind him
Henry heard the high, thrilled cry of a child: Dada
Dada Dada. It was a moment Henry never would
forget, a triumphant moment in which all his senses
shared. It was on this that his mind dwelt when he
lay dying over forty years later: the Master's last
vision was of his joy upon an English cricket field
one sunny afternoon in his youth.

It was this vision (deeply hidden of coure) which lay
behind Tzara's selection, and we dare not now say
random selection, of the word Dada on 6 February
1916. Yet deeper, at the very heart of the vision, lies
another and almost bizarre conjunction. Undoubtedly the aesthetical fates (who *do* attend such births
and wield the forceps to good purpose) were present
at the genesis of Dada, for the child who shouted at
the flash of the leaping horse's brass, and he was but
a baby being one year old that very day, was the

84

precocious Marcel Proust. What was he doing in his pram on Chislehurst Common that afternoon? Not only that. What was his father Dr Adrien Proust doing in the windmill just above and behind him?

It is a long (and dull) story; so we will be short. The new French government had prevailed upon the distinguished doctor, some say by a form of blackmail so obscure that none has unravelled it, to organise, under the alias of Edwin Levy (the name was their unpleasant invention) and in the guise of a private detective, a network of spies to observe the old Emperor, whom it still feared, and who had so recently awarded Dr Proust the *Légion d'Honneur*. One of their observation posts was the windmill from where the entrance to Camden Place could be readily taken in view. Observing from it that day, seeing things for himself, was the admirable Dr Proust; with him was his young wife and their son, on a visit and disliking every minute of their stay in the draughty room – 'like a greenhouse', complained Madame Proust, 'all these large windows and that glass-fronted bookcase' – Dr Proust had found for them at nearby Lamorbey Park, Sidcup. So it was that Proust *père* looking on, Proust *fils*, astonished by the brilliant light from the rocking horse, cried out his curious yet unmistakable Dada, and Henry James, the moment's hero, was transfixed. And so it was too that when Tristan Tzara said the word in the Café de la Terrasse that evening in 1916 there was more to Dada than had met his eye.

8

The True Story of Captain Oates

THE SECRET of Captain Oates has been well kept. Accident has aided design in this, for the death of Captain Scott and his two companions, Edward Wilson and Birdie Bowers, in March 1912 was not part of the plan to put a British secret agent into the Imperial German Navy. Because of the way they died the fiction, which they had concocted during the last marches across the Ross Ice Shelf, of a Captain Oates walking out to a sacrificial death, was never questioned; his tragedy was subsumed into theirs as the nation mourned its loss and rejoiced at having such heroes. Even though Oates' body was not found, no one sought to question the story which Scott's diary told; indeed, in such circumstances none thought to.

Now, however, when these British heroes are coming under the scrutiny of clever men out to make names for themselves, and the truth is in danger of being perverted, the story of Scott's last Antarctic expedition and its real objective ought to be told. The record should be put straight, and Scott's failure (to reach the Pole first, to bring the Polar party back safely) at last be seen in the context of the success of his journey South. Moreover, much has been made of the competition between Scott and Amundsen, and so much recently of Scott's deficiencies as leader, that it is high time their cooperation and Scott's skill in making a complicated plan and carrying it out be put before the world. As also there is considerable discussion of Scott's selfishness, into that debate should be put the significant fact of his renunciation of being first at the Pole, a renunciation made before he left London. This sorrow he had to carry alone until autumn 1911; it was a burden he bore bravely and well, for even Bowers did not suspect that the Pole was only a side-show. Finally, Kathleen Scott's name has to be cleared. The average mind of the second half of the twentieth century, it seems, always leaps to a sexual conclusion; like that unaverage mind of the twelfth century, St. Bernard's, it believes a man and a woman alone in a room – in this case one of them, Kathleen Scott, lying on a sofa – cannot help themselves fornicating. As we shall see, Nansen and Mrs. Scott were up to something else in the Hotel Westminster in late January 1912: as Scott struggled back from the Pole, his part of the plot successfully completed, they in Berlin were putting the finishing touches to their part of the same plot, a plot so remarkable that Erskine Childers or John Buchan could have invented it. Perhaps they did. We know that J.M. Barrie was involved, and if he had a hand in it why not them?

The plan was hatched when two things happened. The dead body of a young German seaman was discovered in the sea off Harwich, and the Admiralty became convinced that it needed an agent not just inside the German navy but on board one of the battleships in the High Seas Fleet. At the same time a second expedition to the Antarctic under Captain

Scott was being prepared. It took Barrie's genius to put together the scheme which combined these diverse components. Many of the details still remain hidden; not all the documents have come to light, no doubt many were destroyed and probably much was never committed to paper. We do not know, for example, where Birdie Bowers recruited Captain Oates. Bowers had long been a secret agent, Oates had for long been dissatisfied with his life as a cavalry soldier. Thus a lone soldier among sailors went South with Scott, and one anomaly at least is explained. Also the Norwegian end of the story is hazy. Why was it considered essential to get Oates into the German navy through Norway? When was Nansen brought into it? Who suggested that coordination with Amundsen and a race for the South Pole between him and Scott be the means to achieve the desired end? Was that Barrie? It was so extravagant an adventure for such a mundane purpose one is tempted to think it was.

Not knowing all the answers to these and other questions it is also a temptation to over-estimate the degree of planning involved; perhaps we should bear in mind some measure, possibly large, of improvisation. Much eventually went wrong. Even in 1917 in the High Seas Fleet the Admiralty failed to work everything out and Oates this time became a real, rather than the imaginary, sacrifice he had been in 1912. So no doubt some things which had not been prepared for went right. The cardboard replica of Oates, for instance, was a last minute makeshift solution to a problem which had defeated the best minds in the Admiralty, yet so well did it do its job no one has suggested that Oates never was at the South Pole. The pity is that its creator, Birdie Bowers, did not live to see how perfectly his invention worked.

The timing of Oates' transference to Amundsen was, nonetheless, the most important matter to get right. Lengthy negotiations were out of the question once both expeditions were in Antarctica, so the day had to be set as soon as Amundsen arrived at the Bay of Whales. It was chosen by Amundsen according to the schedules he had already worked out, and Scott soon realized that he would have to delay his own progress South if he were to be going when Amundsen was coming back. It was one of the reasons for giving up the huskies. The rendezvous on Christmas Day 1911 at the top of the Beardmore Glacier meant a detour for Amundsen, but for Scott it meant dawdling across the Ross Ice Shelf. Going slow was best done on foot: man haulage was the British corollary of the Norwegians' dog teams.

That historic rendezvous has never been described. We have to imagine the jubilant Norwegians arriving while the British were eating their horse meat stew, and the surprise of all save Scott and Bowers at their carrying off Oates when they departed. The surprise must soon have given way to despondency, both on the part of the last support party (Teddy Evans, Crean and Lashly) who were shortly to return, and on the part of Wilson and Edgar Evans, who were to go on to the Pole with Scott – for Scott was determined that there should be no deception on that score. On their return journey Teddy Evans' habitual buoyancy collapsed, and the account of how Crean and Lashly got him back safely deservedly ranks among the greatest of stories of endurance, courage and resourcefulness. We know too how badly Edgar Evans took it. Wilson's composure was not disturbed; for him, as for Bowers, this was a quality to be cultivated in all conditions; indeed, the tougher the going got the more cheerful should one become. Scott suffered most. Even though he had lived longest with the knowledge that the last 250 miles to the Pole would be purposeless, when the fact stared him in the face, and he, Wilson, Bowers and Edgar Evans set off across the plateau with Oates in cardboard shape aboard their sledge, something in him rebelled. It took all Wilson and Bowers' strength of mind and sense of the absurd to keep him from giving way; his diary shows how successful they were.

Oates himself, we have to assume, was delighted to be going off with the Norwegians. There was no longer the lure of being first at the Pole to draw him on; besides, when Amundsen had appeared Oates had not been sure that Scott would take him in the Polar party. For it was Bowers, at that time a member of Teddy Evans' support party, who seemed to Oates to be more in Scott's confidence than he was; Oates was, therefore, doubtful about his own place in the team which would make the dash to the Pole. All had now been made clear: Bowers had to join Scott's party because Oates was being carried off by Amundsen. What hitherto has seemed a strange, because gratuitously dangerous, decision of Scott's, to take five men on the last lap and to reduce the returning party to three, is also made clear to us. He took four, and there were only three to send back, for the other one was already on the first stage of his journey to Europe.

Once Oates had been carried away, and the support party had gone, the remaining miles for the Polar party must have been very long. All of them were ignorant of what Oates' role was to be in the war they knew was coming; probably if they had been told they would have looked happier in those famous photographs taken at the Pole. Wilson and Bowers can manage a smile, even a chuckle, for the comicality of being photographed beside the cardboard Oates did not escape them. But Scott and Evans are grim.

Evans, as on the homeward journey he became more and more ill, grew everyday more dejected. By the time the party arrived at the foot of the Beardmore Glacier, frostbite, inadequate rations and bitter disappointment had so eroded Evans' confidence that his will to live gave way. Beside his body Wilson, Bowers and Scott buried the replica of Oates; unable to destroy it at the Pole for reasons they found it hard to explain to each other, they realized now that its extra weight (added to that of their rock samples) would be the certain death of them. As they trudged ever more slowly across the Ross Ice Shelf what sustained them each weary night was the invention of Oates' death. It was a joint undertaking, and it took shape gradually. If it was Wilson who saw most clearly what Oates should be said to have done, it was Scott who choose the phrases that described it, and Bowers who produced those simple words of Oates which will never be forgotton: 'I am just going outside and may be some time.' By the end of February they had the story complete and began to write it up. But by the time they committed Oates to his heroic end, their own case had become desperate. Thereafter Scott was writing the hopeless truth, and in the unrelenting blizzards of late March he, Wilson and Bowers died eleven miles short of One Ton Depot.

By then Oates was in Sydney. He had arrived at Hobart in the *Fram* on 7 March, had been taken to Australia in a British frigate, and was due to leave for Bergen on 1 April. There he disappears from view. He reappears late in 1912 as Albin Köbis, a stoker in the *Prinzregent Luitpold*. Mrs. Scott and Nansen had made the right contacts in Berlin earlier in the year, and no one suspected Albin Köbis of being other than a man who had knocked about the world a good deal in the German merchant navy before deciding to join the Imperial Fleet. All, therefore, seemed to have gone smoothly. Even the news of Scott and his companions' deaths, which reached London in February 1913, though it shocked the Lords of the Admiralty as much as it shocked anyone, had for them a great advantage: no one now could conceive of Oates dying other than in the manner he was said to have done in Scott's journal. No one, that is, except Oates' mother.

It was Bowers who had kept Oates' diary after Oates had left on 25 December. He had known Oates best and it had seemed to him not a difficult task to imitate Oates' terse entries. Nor was it, and it crossed no one's mind to suspect them counterfeit. Not even at the time Mrs Oates. Only as time passed and she read and reread the diary did she begin to have doubts. By then 1917 had come and gone, and the war was over; when she mentioned her suspicions and became openly critical of Scott she was told the truth. Subsequently she destroyed the diary. What she was told cannot have comforted her.

If this really were a story by Buchan, Köbis-Oates would have performed some daring exploit which would have turned the tide of war against the Germans. At a critical moment a view-finder would have jammed, a stopcock been opened, a crucial message not been sent. No such moment occured. The Admiralty had put Oates-Köbis in the wrong place. He was probably quicker to realize this than they were; in August 1917, however, it was decided that if he was to be of any use the time had come. As the decisive action to defeat the German High Seas Fleet was not to be made on the high seas, it would have to be taken in port. The discontent of the sailors with their rations and with their officers was at a height; Oates-Köbis reluctantly led them in a determined protest.

On the morning of 2 August six hundred of the seven hundred sailors of the *Prinzregent Luitpold* walked off their ship at Wilhelmshaven. It was a mistake. They were premature and were not joined by the crews of other vessels. When they returned to the *Prinzregent Luitpold* a little later that day stoker Albin Köbis was arrested. After a court-martial he was found guilty of mutiny, and at 7.03 a.m. on 5 September 1917 at the Wahn Firing Range near Cologne, Captain Laurence Edward Grace Oates was executed by firing squad.

9

Lo. Lee. Ta.

THIS MORNING I took my children to the swimming
baths at Newcastle-under-Lyme. It was a celebration: seventy-three years ago, on 22 October 1906,
the baths were opened. In the entrance hall hangs a
photograph taken at the opening, and I noticed, as I
had not before, three figures on the chute at the deep
end. They were the celebrities of the day, but few
would recognise them now: acrobatic swimming has
long been out of fashion. Yet *Les Malouins*, as they
called themselves, were the best and the opening of
the largest bath in the English Midlands deserved
the best; Frank Tilton, the baths superintendant,
considered the expense of getting them well worth-
while. Riboulet, the experienced old sailor who had
twice been shipwrecked off Cape Horn, was their
leader; it was he who had caught and trained the
albatross Chateaubriand which played so lively a
role in their performance. Auguste Menard and
Lucien Humbert were much younger men and therefore more agile; upon them the greater part of the
show depended. Their display was brilliant, but it
was not their remarkable swimming which came to
mind when I recognised them this morning; prob-

ably because Lucien was seated most prominently on the chute, what I remembered was his little-known literary achievement.

Auguste's brother Pierre fired Lucien's enthusiasm. Jorge Luis Borges has made Pierre's name immortal and the task he attempted justly famous. It was to compose *Don Quixote*. As Borges comments: 'To be, in some way, Cervantes and to arrive at *Don Quixote* seemed to him less arduous – and consequently less interesting – than to continue being Pierre Menard and to arrive at *Don Quixote* through the experiences of Pierre Menard'. It was a magnificent vision, an heroic endeavour. Lucien's undertaking was no less quixotic. It was, it had to be, equally arduous. For generations Humberts and Menards have lived as friendly rivals in St. Malo, the intensity of the competition never underminding their affection, which has survived between the families long after particular victories and defeats have been forgotten: none of them knows now whether it was a Menard or a Humbert who named with such deftness *la rue du chat qui danse*.

Once Auguste had told Lucien of his brother's great task Lucien was no longer to be seen behind the counter of his wine ship in the cathedral square – bought with the profits of *Les Malouins*' successful tours in those halcyon pre-war days, when a display in Staffordshire and the gold medal in the water games at Zug were all in a season's work. He was now to be observed tramping the ramparts, gazing at the sea, or, as if imitating recent art, seated on his favourite bench, chin cupped in hand, thinking. His idea, when it came was audacious. He would not go back but forward. To remain Lucien Humbert, but to arrive at not just the book but also its author: to compose both writer and novel. He pondered the possibilities. Nothing straightforward would do;

Pierre had to be thoroughly outmatched. Lucien watched the sun go down, a vivid red beachball falling into a metal sea; a yacht with fuchsia sails drifted harbourwards, he turned homewards too. I need not here describe all the candidates Lucien created, considered, and discarded during those delicious Spring days of 1924. It was not until early June that he had the man he wanted clear.

In October 1948 Malcolm and Margerie Lowry visited St. Malo. The town *intra muros* was still in ruins from the battle fought there in the first fortnight of August 1944. Lowry stumbling about 'the terrible shell' of the cathedral was neither too sick nor too drunk to overlook the notice which had been posted in the vestry, nor to fail to make a note of it: *Vous oui passez avez pitié d'une paroisse totalement sinistre par le Fer et par le Feu ... aidons nous, merci.* Nor did he fail to take note of the paper wrapped around the bottle of gin he had purchased at a wine shop facing him all too temptingly when he came out of the west door of the cathedral. Seated beside the statue of Jacques Cartier – 'like me he discovered Canada, only from the other direction', said Lowry – he and Margerie drank the gin and examined the paper. On it they read:

> the Hummer. Time: Sunday morning in June. Place: Sunlit living room. Props: old candy-striped davenport, magazines, phonograph, Mexican knick-knacks (the late Mr. Harold E. Haze- God bless the good man – had engendered my darling at the siesta hour in a blue-washed room, on a honeymoon trip to Vera Cruz, and mementoes, among these Dolores, were all over the place). She wore that day

We do not know if Lowry recognised his fragment when in due course it appeared in Paris in 1955, embedded in the book which he may not even have read before his death in 1957. Nor do we know how much of his book Lucien wrote, or, put another way, how many bottles were wrapped in his work before his daughter-in-law, for she it was who served Malcolm Lowry, had to look elsewhere for her supply of paper than her father-in-law's desk. Lucien was not there to prevent this disposal of his great literary enterprize; being the man he was, he would probably have enjoyed its dispersal in this random way to the good folk of his native city, some topers getting (who knows) whole chapters. Nor was Auguste there to be able to do anything about it. Both men had been killed fighting for the freedom of their beloved St. Malo. Their names are inscribed side by side on the war memorial in the *Place des Frères Lamennais*. That is one way of commemorating them; this piece is another.

22 October 1979   in memory of the people of St. Malo who died in the war, 1939–1945.

10

Anna Blume in England

THE QUEST began in Ambleside cemetery. I had just
put a few late crysanthemums on Kurt Schwitters'
grave when I noticed the name Louise Flitters on a
neighbouring tombstone. That name seemed familiar; where had I encountered it before? I could not
remember. Schwitters-Flitters: I repeated the mes-
meric incantation as I walked back into the grey
stone town, drawing stares of disapproval. Undeter-
red I continued to chant (Flitters-Schwitters) and to
ponder. There had to be a connection, I knew there
had been. Yet what it was escaped me.

On the long journey home I began to shed my
preoccupation. By the time Crewe arrived I was
merely irritating my fellow travellers, at Euston I
drew barely a glance so murmurous had my Flitters-
Schwitters become, and when I reached Sidcup no
one noticed my faint whispering, not even the vicar,
with his ear attuned for the soft word, as I put down
my suitcase in the church porch. I went to my usual
distant pew, where as a boy I had sat at confirmation
classes. I had always come here since to recapture
the perfect boredom of those Spring evenings; this
place soothed and never failed to restore me to a

ready acceptance of the nonsense of my daily life. No Schwitters-Flitters flickered now as I stared at the memorial to the Great War dead which served as the reredos to this familiar side altar; the golden-lettered Sidcup names had finally erased its obsessive magic. Richards, Quarterman, Ayres, Pinter, del Néro, Humbert, von Poellnitz – von Poellnitz! I sprang up: that strange name among all the mundane anonymous others had brought me back to Schwitters. The vicar put his head out of the vestry; you alright he asked. Perfectly I replied. Major H.W. von Poellnitz, Royal Flying Corps: I banged my prayer book on the altar rail (the vicar's head popped out again, a more concerned expression on his face). Of course, I cried, not Louise but Victoria. Victoria? the vicar was puzzled. He never had been able to follow my trains of thought. That's who it had been. Victoria Flitters had married Hannibal von Poellnitz, and Hannibal von Poellnitz was the name Schwitters had mentioned to Stefan Themerson in 1947. I could recall the exact quotation. At Maida Vale one bleak coalless afternoon in February of that terrible winter Kurt, wrapped up in his Norwegian sweater, had volunteered that von Poellnitz was the greatest influence on his art; *'auf meinem Artz ist Hannibal von Poellnitz der grossen influenz'* were the very words according to Themerson, who had at first thought Kurt was referring to his streaming cold and had gone to fetch a Beecham's Powder. He, like all other *literateurs* and literary scholars since, had been bemused by Kurt's almost unique reference to influences upon his work. Tantalized indeed, for 'who was von Poellnitz' had become the question asked in countless discussions at numberless colloquia on 'Dada: its place in our culture' in the universities of the western world even until now. And here I stood

100

transfixed in the north aisle of Holy Trinity, Sidcup,
Kent with the answer in golden writing before me. I
was sure of that: H.W. was Hannibal alright. Yet my
instinctive certainty would not convince sceptical
professors or yearning postgraduate students.
Where was the evidence?

Perhaps the vicar could help after all. I burst into
the vestry. He was poring over the suburban timet-
able. I brushed aside his attempt to discourse on the
virtues of the Dartford Loop line and begged him to
tell me did Victoria von Poellnitz still live. I knew
much, perhaps everything, hung on his reply. Yes he
said. Where, where I babbled. He looked more and
more alarmed. 105 Burnt Oak Lane he said. It was
my turn to stare for that was only a few doors away
from my own home. But she hasn't been out for
years, he quickly went on seeing my astonishment,
not since you were confirmed. I remember it so well,
he continued, because she and the bishop talked for
so long afterwards. You remember Dr. Chavasse,
the bishop of Rochester, don't you? I overheard him
say to her it was her doing that he'd gone into the
Church: if she chooses von Poellnitz damn it I'll
become a priest. He stood there waving a viennese
whorl in one hand, his cup of tea in the other. I
couldn't stop to hear more, though their animation
was striking, because the Pinter boy had been sick
all over the carpet. You remember *him* surely?

Can I see her I asked, wondering whether the
Bishop of Rochester's heroic exploits in that atro-
cious war might have been the consequence of his
unrequited passion for the lady I was desperate to
see. How love denied gets things done I thought,
recalling the row of us at the sunny altar rail, his
heavy episcopal hands on each of us in turn. Of
course, the vicar replied, relieved now to observe my
excitement taking a normal course, she's as sane as

101

you or I, she just doesn't go out that's all. I take her the eucharist every week. Why don't you come with me tomorrow when I go?

That then is how it came about. I had never put the necessary two and two together before: my major H.W. von Poellnitz was Schwitters' Hannibal. The connection had been there plainly before me all those years, yet it had taken a visit to Ambleside and the casual glimpse of another gravestone for me to arrive at this crucial point. Still, I reflected, isn't that how knowledge advances: by accident?

I waited at the front door of 105 Burnt Oak Lane the following morning with an anticipation border-ing on impatience. We went upstairs and into the back room. There was not the slightest reminiscence of Miss Havisham here; in that light and airy room the sturdy Mrs. von Poellnitz gave us a cheerful welcome which was almost vivacious. She was, she said, pleased to meet me. After communion and the vicar's departure, and when the coffee had been brought by her niece and companion Miss Tait, I asked her about Louise. Yes, she said, her sister had died in a climbing accident in the Lake District. Oh, that had been many, many years ago. No, Kurt Schwitters she'd never heard of. If he was a friend of her husband's it hadn't been during their year of marriage which, naturally, she remembered in almost every detail. She smiled and poured me another cup of coffee. But I knew, didn't I, that he had been a prisoner of war, perhaps he had met my Kurt Schwitters — it was Schwitters wasn't it — then? Where had he been a prisoner I asked her. At many places she said, she couldn't remember them all, though as she had all his letters she could soon tell me. None of the places she read out meant much to me or could have done to Schwitters, I thought, as she put down the last but one of the little packet of

letters. Then, she sighed, they took him all the way
to a hospital in Hanover when they decided to
amputate his leg. That's where he wrote this last
letter to me. My flagging confidence that I was on
the right track revived at once. Might I read that
letter I asked, explaining that Hanover was Kurt
Schwitters' city. She said I might. There wasn't
anything in it that was embarrassing she thought;
young married folk in 1917 weren't as explicit as
they are nowadays. I skimmed the first two para-
graphs with their censored sentiments and came to
the third which began:

'This might amuse you. There's a curious fellow who
visits us here, some clerk or other from Army Head-
quarters in town I think he must be. Comes to check on
us I wouldn't wonder. Yesterday he turned up while I
was stumping about the ward declaiming poetry – to
keep our spirits up you know with a bit of dear old
England. Odd poems they are the map instructor fellow
gave me on that course I had to take. You remember me
telling you about him. Anyhow, I was just starting on a
poem about a farmyard when this army clerk arrived.
He stood there listening and when I'd finished he ran
up to Mary – one of the splendid nurses we have here –
and started jumping up and down, throwing his arms
about and waving his cap, and talking at the top of his
voice. The whole ward stopped to watch him. The
upshot was Mary came to ask me, as she speaks some
English, to read the poem once more as her friend just
had to hear it again. No one else minded so I read it out
again. He slapped his hands against his legs and
danced about. Do you know the queer fish had me read
that poem out half-a-dozen times. Then he came over
and shook my hand. Now isn't that strange? I wonder
what he liked so much about an English farmyard?'

When I handed the letter back to Mrs. von Poellnitz
I was trembling. So I should have been, for I was on
the edge of solving one of the most baffling, one of

the greatest literary mysteries of our time. Here it was: the thirty-year old Kurt's moment of artistic vision, a vision which thereafter would never fail him. 1917, everyone knows, was the year he started writing his own poems, the year his pictures began to be composed out of the odds and ends of our civilization – come to think of it, what by 1917 was left of our civilization but odds and ends? He had understood that just as perfectly as those other Dadaists had understood it the year before in Zurich, but his understanding (I felt sure) had been born as he listened to that poem in a Hanover hospital ward. What a crux in the history of Art the reading of that poem was: the birthday of *Merz*. I got up and looked out into the garden, seeing nothing.

Nor was the poem von Poellnitz's, though Kurt had always thought so; it had been written by a British map instructor. I hardly dared to think it but the thought could not be prevented, for only one British poet had been a map instructor. I barely heard Mrs. von Poellnitz speaking. I struggled back to the suburban realities of that Sidcup back room: coffee spoons and the brown oval photograph over the mantlepiece. He wasn't shot down you know (she was saying), the engine failed or something; silly really; and his death was another accident that nurse said, the wrong dressing on his leg. She came all the way to tell me how bravely he had died, and what a good man he had been. That was kind of her. She hadn't come all the way from Germany, but from somewhere near Lowestoft or Yarmouth; she'd married one of her English patients, a doctor I think, and come back with him after the war. She was a very nice girl. Mrs. von Poellnitz sat still.

I knew I ought to go, and I hesitated a little before I asked her what I absolutely had to. I spoke quietly: did they send you his things? From Hanover you mean she answered: no, but the nurse brought what little there was, for there wasn't much. Would you like to see? I offered up a short prayer to those muses who had ensured that Victoria von Poellnitz was the very opposite of Juliana Bordereau, and said I would.

I saw the poem at once. A tattered fragment and just the one. Yes, that's all the poems, she said, when I looked up quizzically. Its in Hannibal's hand. I knew the poem.

Immediately I realized its significance for Kurt and thus for the history of modern culture. The poem's celebration of discarded things, even of useless things, I understood at once was what Kurt in the chaos of 1917 was clapping his hands and dancing for. Mrs. von Poellnitz asked me and I told her who had written it. Ah yes, she said, that was when Hannibal was at the camp at Gidea Park; that was, let me see, April 1916 – that's where they would have met. But do read me the poem; I would like to hear it. She sat upright and alert. I read:

Tall nettles cover up, as they have done
These many springs, the rusty harrow, the plough
Long worn out, and the roller made of stone:
Only the elm butt tops the nettles now.

This corner of the farmyard I like most:
As well as any bloom upon a flower
I like the dust on the nettles, never lost
Except to prove the sweetness of a shower.

Dust on the nettles I sofly repeated when I'd finished. That's it you see. That's it exactly. And will you write about it, she asked; its important isn't it? I nodded. How startled the academic world would be when it appeared. What should I call it? The origin of *Merz*? Who was von Poellnitz: a riddle solved? Too flashy I considered. The influence of Edward Thomas on Kurt Schwitters? Too dry. Edward Thomas and Kurt Schwitters: an unlooked for connection disclosed? Yes, that would do very well. Profuse in my thanks I stood up to go; as I did so I knocked the little heap of von Poellnitz's effects from the arm of the chair. A photograph fell face upwards on the carpet. I recognised the girl's face, just as earlier I had recognised that of Hannibal von Poellnitz over the fireplace. Oh, that's the nurse, said Mrs. von Poellnitz; she left me her picture; don't you think she was handsome? I believe she wrote her name on the back for me. I turned it over: Mary Baumgartener it read. Isn't it an odd name for a British doctor, Mrs. von Poellnitz said. No stranger than von Poellnitz for a British airman I replied. She laughed and shook my hand.

I left 105 Burnt Oak Lane exuberant. And yet. I stopped short in my skipping along the road. And yet I'd never asked her what von Poellnitz was doing in Sidcup, how his exotic name had come to be among those of local families like the del Néros, the Humberts or the Pinters, all of whom had, I knew, been resident in the district for generations. That's how it always is I thought. The obvious always gets overlooked: just as no one had seen the obvious artistic conjunction of Edward Thomas's poetry and Kurt Schwitters' art. How blind the experts are. I skipped elatedly on.

There is an epilogue. After the publication of my paper and the furore it aroused, the interviews with the press, the public readings, the famous television programme, I was not surprised to be offered the Chair of Literature at one of the more distinguished universities. When I returned this year to place the flowers on Kurt's grave – twenty pence worth of discarded and disregarded blooms for Michaelmas – I was no more startled to see just behind his austere stone another, equally severe, with a name I knew upon it. I had checked Kurt's paintings and found what I had been looking for in his masterly *Das Bäumerbild* of 1920: Hannibal von Poellnitz and Mary Baumgartener staring out at me. For she, the nurse, and he, the poetry reading prisoner of war, had been to Kurt alike in their inspiration. It was she who was Anna Blume, forever in his poetry, named I knew now from that sixth line of Edward Thomas's poem, 'As well as any bloom upon a flower'. Eve Blossom he had called her in English, but Mary Baumgartener she had become, and perhaps he knew that too. The military clerk would have been no match for a British doctor. Or would he? For that neighbouring tombstone simply read: Mary Baumgartener, Gorleston-on-Sea, 8 March 1948. Two months to the day after Kurt had died his beloved Anna Blume too had died and here in Ambleside, far from breezy Gorleston-on-Sea. I turned away up the path. Even I, I reflected, should leave this mystery a mystery. After all I had my professorship now.

11

A Suffolk Mystery

'When one reads his books, one doesn't feel that he, that he could have known the people if he met them in the street'.

'I think Henry James was a great master of situations, in a sense, of his plot, but his characters hardly exist outside the story'.

'They have definite goals, but they never attain them ... The moment you know that the man is after the Aspern papers, you know, well, either that he'll never find the papers, or that if he does find them, they'll be worthless ... its also an ambiguity. For example, 'The Turn of the Screw'. That's a stock example'.

from Richard Burgin,
Conversations with Jorge Luis Borges,
(Discus Books, New York, 1970), pp. 70, 74.

THE FIRST encounter occurred in Saxmundham High Street. Henry had bicycled from Dunwich where he has staying with his cousins during August 1897. Miss Jessel had come down the short flight of steps at the entrance to the *Bell Hotel*; Henry had just swung round the corner from the Market Place.

They did not actually bump into each other, but a hesitantly performed dance of intricate steps took place with Henry removing his cap and Miss Jessel fluttering her hands in the air. Neither spoke. Then they passed on. Henry, after a rapid inspection of the town whose rustic activity thoroughly satisfied the expectations aroused in him by what he called its 'Old Hodge' name, to Yoxford, Miss Jessel to the station to meet the London train.

The second encounter was in the garden of The White Horse, Westleton. Henry had been tempted by the Crown, its open doorway displaying a vista through a dim passageway of a shadowy yard beyond, but he had cycled on to the green and, dismounting, had gone in through the gate to the sunlit and flowery garden of the modern public house. His pint of beer and a plate of sandwiches were brought out to him; he ate and looked about. Miss Jessel and her companion were at no great distance to his left seated beneath a tree. He did not attend to their conversation; it drifted to him in snatches. Later he would recall her animation, the young man's unusually large, long face, his passivity as she regarded him, and that their discussion had been of the Grand National and the St. Moritz Tobogganing Club.

The third encounter was at Southwold. Henry had had his tea and was cycling along the cliff path on his way to the harbour and the ferry which would carry him across the river to Walberswick and so home to his dinner at Dunwich. They were sitting on a fishing boat below him on the beach. Clouds had hidden the sun and in the gusty breeze the sea was beating whitely on the shingle. It was Miss Jessel's red dress which caught Henry's attention; she was still talking and her companion listening intently. Henry did not stop, but rode on past the Fishermens'

Reading Room and across Gun Hill. Miss Jessel and
Bertie Dwyer soon got up and left too; they went in
the opposite direction, to the station where they took
the little train of the Southwold Railway to Hales-
worth and their connection for Saxmundham and
London.

We know the day on which these encounters
occurred because Wilson Steer always precisely
dated his pictures. His painting of fishing boats on
Southwold beach, at the City Art Gallery, York,
shows Miss Jessel and Bertie Dwyer as Henry
James cycling by had seen them. Wilson Steer had
waved to him but Henry's attention had been en-
gaged by the pair below; he had noticed neither the
artist nor his companionable greeting.

We know little else. Of course, it is a well-known
fact that the season 1897–8 was one of the greatest,
arguably the most outstanding of that ace of the
Cresta Run, Bertie Dwyer. He won the Grand
National and other cup races as well. His skill
(especially the manner in which he rode through
Shuttlecock), according to the old hands who had
watched him since his astonishing second place in
the Grand National ten years previously when he
was a fourteen-year old schoolboy, was uncanny.
That winter he rode as if he had been bewitched,
Major Bulpett later recalled. How does he do it, was
a question frequently asked in the bar of the Kulm
Hotel after darkness had descended on the Run and
the tobaggoners were discussing the day's sport.
Bertie's rivals were perplexed, one of them, the
powerful rider R.W. 'Cocky' Bird, more than most,
for he maintained that either his toboggan slid out
of control at the most unlikely places – going
through Junction or across the Post Road for instance – or he himself became (as he put it) 'muzzy' at
Top and so lost valuable tenths of a second at the

start. It may be that he or others voiced their suspicions at meetings of the Club. There was a rumour that at one meeting Bertie, having been liberally plied with gin, blurted something out – but what we will never know, for at the end of the season all the records of the Club were 'accidentally' burnt; nothing at all was saved. That too is a well-known fact.

There is nothing else. Miss Jessel seems now no more than a figment of Henry James' imagination, a powerful creation of that powerful instrument; beyond the claustrophobic pages of *The Turn of the Screw* (written in 1898) it is as if she had no life at all.

12
Dung ABC

DUNG A

AMONG the first and last three things we have heard
much recently of bread, less of hay,[1] nothing of
manure. Despite F.W. Maitland's 'the demand for
manure has played a large part in the history of the
human race',[2] despite the clear fact that without it
there would be insufficient bread, Braudel's *Capitalism and Material Life*, a widely read and quite
justifiably influential book, makes no more than
passing reference to manure, yet has a whole section
on bread (rice, maize). In the index to Charles B.
Heiser Jnr's *Seed to Civilization* (1973), subtitled the
story of man's food, fertilizer has a single entry,
dung is not recorded; there is a hint here (I would
suggest) of our scholarly ability to overlook the
obvious; Marc Bloch made that point beautifully in
French Rural History: '. . . some lords demanded
"pots of excrement" as part of their dues, to the great

---

[1] We should note however the splendid chapter on the hay
trade in George Ewart Evans, *The Days That We Have Seen*
(1975), 76–105.
[2] *Domesday Book and Beyond* (Fontana 1960), 106.

113

indignation of some over-sensitive scholars who have mistaken what was merely prudent husbandry for a gross and calculated insult'.[3] Hardheaded lords knew better and not only in France in the Middle Ages; from north China[4] to north Lancashire[5] they, as we would expect, had their priorities so far as these first things mattered, right. Hardheaded peasants had too, since the neolithic revolution turned them into farmers, *c.* 12000 years ago,[6] from Tralee to Timbuctoo, from Tibet to Thamesside. In Ireland, where English colonialism had so whittled life down that its bare bones stuck out for all to see, there was no mistaking the equation; shit equals survival — 'where there is muck there is luck'; so valuable was it you kept it in your living room or just outside your door where it was directly under your eye.[7] From Timbuctoo it was carted and to

[3] English translation 1966, 25.

[4] 'Legendary in the region were the landlords so stingy that they would not allow their hired men to defecate in the fields but made them walk all the way back to the ancestral home to deposit their precious burden': William Hinton, *Fanshen* (Penguin Books 1972), 26.

[5] M.W. Barley, *The House and Home* (1963), plates 210–211: 'houses at Preston, built before 1844 for workers in the cotton mills. They were condemned at that time by a Royal Commission, because of their sanitary arrangements; sewage from earth closets in each enclosed yard (some containing pigsties) flowed in the open sewer between the rows to a cesspool which belonged to the landlord, who emptied it and sold the contents twice a year'.

[6] Herodotus caught the contempt of pastoralists for arable farmers: the king of Ethiopia 'asked what the Persian king ate and what was the greatest age that Persians could attain. Getting in reply an account of the nature and cultivation of wheat, and hearing that the Persian king ate bread, and that people in Persia did not commonly live beyond eighty, he said he was not surprised that anyone who ate dung should die so soon': *The Histories* (Penguin Books revised ed. 1972), 212.

[7] E. Estyn Evans, *Irish Folk Ways* (1957), 100–101; and cf Tom Steel, *The Life and Death of St Kilda* (1975), 81; *The*

Thamesside it was carried by boat to fertilize fields and gardens.[8] In Tibet yak dung served many purposes – for fuel,[9] to keep the wind off, to make ice boxes to store meat, and (mixed with the contents of monastic latrines) as fertilizer.[10] It is of course in China that composting became an art and, in the north at least, where animals were so few, human excrement was precious. No passage of writing so clearly and so tenderly catches the measure of the delicate relationship between men and the land as that of William Hinton's in *Fanshen*, where he describes helping the villagers to plant their grain:

'. . . two others hurriedly scooped out small hollows in the ground. These hollows, each of which was formed with one blow of the hoe, were spaced some three feet apart in rows that were likewise separated by three feet. Into each hollow a generous portion of night soil was poured. The hoe wielders then flung some dirt back over it to form a bed for the seed, and Old Lady Wang herself dropped three seeds – no more, no less – on top of the dirt. To complete the job the seeds were covered with loose earth and lightly tamped in with foot pressure . . .'[11]

Mabinogion, trans. Gwyn Jones and Thomas Jones (Everyman ed. 1949), 137–8.

[8] Actually Kano: see E.C. Curwen and G. Hatt, *Plough and Pasture* (N.Y. 1953), 258, cf Yenan, Jan Myrdal, *Report from a Chinese Village* (Pan Books 1975), 133; for London see E.L. Sabine, 'City Cleaning in Medieval London', *Speculum* XII (1937), 24. This and Sabine's two other papers, 'Latrines and Cesspools of Medieval London', *Speculum* IX (1934), 'Butchering in Medieval London', *Speculum* VIII (1933), ought to be better and more widely known.

[9] Cf Lincolnshire 'where the pig shits soap and the cow shits fire', quoted by Eric Kerridge, *The Farmers of Old England* (1973), 28.

[10] Thubten Jigme and Colin Turnbull, *Tibet* (Penguin Books 1972), 58, 72–3, 74, 262.

[11] *Op. cit.*, 508. Old Lady Wang's 3 seeds might be compared to the 4 seeds in a hole of the English rhyme: the difference is a large one.

We are here brought face to face – I was at any rate – with realities hitherto I had not dreamed of. I can speak of cultural revelation, intellectual shock. For a suburban child (so many of us these days) this was a new awareness of the close connection of shit and food, which to a country boy would be in view daily:

> 'Grampy used to go along there [his "ground"] every night, with a big bath full of pig dung, and then come back with a big bath full of cabbages or whatever was about – potatoes – never came back empty handed – and that's where he got his name, they used to call him "Mucky".'[12]

This connection, once revealed, shows itself everywhere, and dung, so despised in our culture (out of sight out of mind), appears wherever our attention is turned upon that old culture George Ewart Evans has made so vivid for us.[13] On the dung hill and the haystack all depended: for reflective travellers middens and ricks would have been not just the most common features of the landscape, but also the most prominent. Thus our picture is apt: dung hill in the foreground, Dedham church in the distance.[14] Poets as well as painters too: Elynour Rummyng's ale got its flavouring, according to Skelton,[15] from 'the donge of her hennes,

[12] *Village Life and Labour*, ed. Raphael Samuel (1975), 193; cf 200, 'the pig served as both a dustbin and a sewer . . .'.
[13] From *Ask the Fellows who Cut the Hay* (1956) onwards. The recognition this great innovator deserves (but has not received from the academic world at large) is displayed by Alun Howkins in 'Enthusiasms', *History Workshop* I (Spring 1976), 254–6.
[14] Cf *Constable Exhibition Catalogue* (The Tate Gallery 1976), No. 133: 'as has recently been pointed out the men in the foreground are digging out a dung-hill, not a gravel pit as was previously supposed . . .'
[15] John Skelton, *Poems*, ed. R.S. Kinsman (Oxford 1969), 58. I owe this reference to my friend Christopher Harrison.

... Gossyp, come hyder,
This ale shal be thycker
And floure the more quycker;
For, I may telle you,
I learned it of a Jewe
When I began to brewe.'

In that tradition of scatological scurrility comes
Monty Python and the Holy Grail: 'Who's that then?
That must be a king. Why? He hasn't got shit all
over him.'[16] Just so. Chaucer's ploughman 'that
hadde ylaid of dong ful many a fother',[17] Iolo Goch's
farmworker – 'there is no living, no world without
him',[18] the Anglo-Saxon shepherd, whose due was
twelve nights' dung at Christmas,[19] would have
appreciated that one. They, tending their ancestral
dung hills,[20] with dung rakes, midden saws, gripes
and muck-knockers,[21] would have understood (surely) both the Zen answer as to what is Buddha: dried
dung;[22] and their modern Chinese brothers' grasp of

[16] I am grateful to another friend, Charles Townshend, for
telling me of and loaning me the record on which this exchange
occurs.
[17] *The Canterbury Tales*, ed. Thomas Tyrwhitt, n.d., 18.
[18] This marvellous Welsh poem of the fourteenth century
George Ewart Evans has translated and placed at the opening of
his book, *Where Beards Wag All* (1970), 7: 'Enduring is second
nature to him' cf R.S. Thomas 'A Peasant': 'Enduring like a tree
under the curious stars'.
[19] 'Rectitudines Singularum Personarum' in *English Historical Documents*, II, ed. D.C. Douglas and G.W. Greenaway (1953),
815.
[20] As Jean de Meung had it *c.* 1275 speaking of nobles who
had become little more than peasants: 'cil qui sont coustomiers
de maindre es paternex fumiers'; cited by A. Murray, 'Religion
among the Poor in Thirteenth Century France: the testimony of
Humbert de Romans', *Traditio* xxx (1974), 292.
[21] John Vince, *Old Farm Tools* (1974), 5–6; Marie Hartley and
Joan Ingilby, *Life and Tradition in the Yorkshire Dales* (1968),
32 and plates 61–2.
[22] *Zen Flesh, Zen Bones*, compiled by Paul Reps (Penguin
Books 1971), 111.

another, or perhaps the same truth: latrines are a question of politics.[23]

Those European peasants, obliged to fold their animals on the lord's land, to cart his dung for him,[24] or (in the 1870s in Ireland) forced to carry it in creels on their backs as punishment for resisting eviction,[25] – they really *did* have shit all over them – knew all about the politics of manure just as they knew all about its culture. 'Good sons feed your dung heaps' – so they were exhorted by thirteenth century agricultural writers;[26] how would they have responded to 'Good sons feed *our* dung heaps': in other words that communalization of shit which has been such a sensational outcome of China's cultural revolution?

> 'Formerly, before the cultural revolution, the households often used to retain their own human excrement for their own private plots of ground. We don't do that any longer. During the cultural revolution our political awareness has increased . . . Now the households give their human excrement to the vegetable team for compost. And get work-points for it.'[27]

These communal arrangements – no more of those endless quarrels over private latrines and their contents[28] – have produced more vegetables at Liu Ling. They have too, we cannot doubt it, produced a new freedom, that which comes with the responsibil-

[23] Jan Myrdal and Gun Kessle, *China: The Revolution Continued* (Penguin Books 1973), 97.

[24] At Otford, Kent, with their own waggons in 1402–3, long after other servile duties had disappeared: Denis Clarke and Anthony Stoyel, *Otford in Kent* (1975), 83.

[25] David Thomson, *Woodbrook* (Penguin Books 1976), 79.

[26] Georges Duby, *Rural Economy and Country Life in the Medieval West* (Eng. translation 1968), document 30.

[27] Myrdal and Kessle, *op. cit.*, 77.

[28] Hinton, *op. cit.*, 178.

ity of sharing, of looking to the needs of each family, and of understanding the interests of the community. Such freedom the Swiss discovered; their precious commodity was hay: the necessity for agricultural cooperation over mountain pasture and alpine meadow fused them into communities, the communities of the Forest Cantons who threw out their lords and became Switzerland.[29] As with hay so with dung. Our study of each can, must take us a long way, so far in fact that we are bound to say: 'I for one do not lament the passing of social organizations which used the many as a manured soil in which to grow a few graceful flowers of refined culture.'[30]

DUNG B

IN THE AUTUMN of 1974 I had to lecture to first year undergraduates on 'Country Life in the Medieval West'. The title I inherited from the previous year's lecturer. What were the essentials of medieval rural life? How did one communicate them to an overwhelmingly urban or suburban audience? These were the two questions on which I reflected in the days before the lecture. The answer to the first soon

[29] E. Bonjour, H.S. Offler and G.R. Potter, *A Short History of Switzerland* (1952), 14–16, 57, 71. The correlation between agrarian cooperation, strong communities and freedom from exploitation has recently been restated in a stimulating paper by Robert Brenner, 'Agrarian Class Structure and Economic Development in Pre-Industrial Europe', *Past and Present* 70 (Feb. 1976).
[30] Thus Theodosius Dobzhansky, an American biologist, cited by Fernand Braudel, *Capitalism and Material Life 1400–1800* (Fontana English ed. 1974), 124.

became clear. I would need to concentrate on bread, hay and dung. Years before I had called one of the half a dozen lectures I had given on the Middle Ages 'Bread'. No difficulty there, though my subsequent reading led me to think that much of the grain grown in medieval fields was consumed as a gruel or porridge[1] rather than as bread.[2] So far as hay was concerned, I had steadily been made aware of its importance by writers on rural life and had come to understand that civilization in the West depended upon the haystack.[3] Dung was not much written about.[4] Nonetheless, I soon realized that without the

---

[1] Most recently described by H.E. Hallam, *Rural England 1066–1348* (1981), p. 65 and by Eugen Weber, *Peasants into Frenchmen, the modernization of rural France 1870–1914* (Paperback ed. 1979), p. 131: *la soupe*. Note the interesting supposition of M.M. Postan, *The Medieval Economy and Society* (Penguin Books 1975), p. 224: 'Porridge and gruel were the commonest family dishes |southern England *c.* 1300| and it is quite possible that some of the porridge was taken as 'brose', as it was to be by Scottish crofters in modern times, i.e. uncooked.'

[2] The culture of bread could be taken a great deal further. Compare Weber, *op. cit.*, pp. 135–7, esp. p. 136, 'the black and indigestible bread, base of the daily diet, was an object of veneration, never cut into until the sign of the cross was carved on it with a knife', with Pierre-Jakez Hélias, *The Horse of Pride, life in a Breton village* (English translation 1978), p. 226–228 and esp. 256–7: 'A peasant would cut his chunk straight from the loaf; he did not like being served slices that had been cut in advance. He enjoyed smelling his bread between bites, chewing it slowly and peacefully, moving it from one side of his mouth to the other before swallowing. And you had to see the attentive expression on his face and the look of concentration in his eyes while he was indulging. It was almost like celebrating Mass – the Mass of our daily bread. Indeed!' Indeed. Moreover, surely the culture of peasant costume (*ibid.* pp. 275–9) requires more attention than I am aware it has been given.

[3] 'Who has hay has bread', says the French proverb: Weber, *op. cit.*, p. 121.

[4] There has subsequently been a perceptive paragraph in J.L. Bolton, *The Medieval English Economy, 1150–1500* (1980), p. 340; cf A.R. Bridbury, 'Sixteenth-Century Farming', *Economic History Review*, 2nd series, xxvii (1974), p. 545.

dung of animals, whom hay sustained during the grassless winters, there would have been no bread. These, therefore, were the three interconnected essentials of rural life, indeed of life itself in medieval Europe: hay, dung and bread (or porridge).

Late in the evening of the day before I had to give the lecture it dawned on me how I ought to present these three basic elements of medieval culture if they were to be firmly and permanently perceived by the audience. It was as an 'equation' that they should be displayed and then expounded: 'Hay equals Dung equals Bread'. And, as initial impact is nine-tenths of the effectiveness of these lectures, it struck me that a certain showmanship would not be misplaced. The following morning I strode into the lecture theatre and wrote in large letters on the blackboard 'SHIT', only adding to it after the perplexed laughter had died away the words 'Hay' (on one side) and 'Porridge' (on the other). Thus the first Hay = Shit = Porridge lecture began.[5]

For the next two or three years I gave the same lecture, but concentrated increasingly on dung (as I came to discover more about its culture), and under the revised title of 'Dung'. An unhappy professor had rejected, on the grounds that the University's reputation would suffer, my proffered title of 'Shit'. After a few years and despite its remoulding the lecture, like any other, needed to be put aside. I turned to other subjects ('War', 'Prayer') and handed the rural economy over to someone else. Something, nonetheless, needed to be done with it, for dung, so far as I could see, was neglected in studies of the medieval economy. In this respect, and only in this respect did I come to have something in common with Marc

[5] The lecture ended, I recall, with a distribution of Westphalian pumpernickel.

Bloch, who had no patience with historians 'who consider the facts of agricultural practices beneath their dignity and who hold their noses as they pass by manure heaps.'[6] Therefore I wrote at Easter 1977 the piece which is published unaltered above. It was written with a distinguished academic journal in mind and I duly sent it there; after two years' consideration the editors decided it was a parody; I am still waiting to hear that they have rejected it. The editors of other academic journals have been speedier in their rejections. Evidently, there is both a narrowness of mind as well as a taboo[7] to be observed here. Academics are, and it is a truism, the last to see what is important. Vladimir Ilych Lenin was one who understood that, and after the treatment my little paper has received I am inclined to agree with his pronouncement of 15 September 1919 that 'The Intelligensia are not the nation's brains but shit'.[8]

I do not fully agree with him: he is wrong about shit. It was not, even in post-revolutionary Russia, contemptible stuff. Yet it is the very stuff of the coinage of contempt. There is a puzzle here,[9] which

[6] Quoted by R.R. Davies, 'Marc Bloch', *History* LII (1967), p. 273.

[7] Margaret Spufford, *Small Books and Pleasant Histories* (1981), p. 193. Note, as a contribution to the subject, Dr Spufford's discovery of the outside privy at Castle-top Farm near Matlock in Derbyshire where there 'is space underneath to back a cart so that it can be easily emptied and the contents used on the fields' (*ibid.*).

[8] Alexander Solzhenitsyn, *The Gulag Archipelago*, I (Fontana 1974), p. 328. In fact, 'shit' was much needed in Russia in Lenin's time, for 'the miserably low' productivity of Eastern European feudal agriculture (particularly on the demesnes) had been due to a lack of fodder, and thus of livestock: Perry Anderson, *Passages from Antiquity to Feudalism* (Verso ed. 1978), pp. 261–2.

[9] See Margaret Spufford, *op. cit.*, p. 185.

is neither a modern nor an urban one. St Francis, for instance, who like Lenin so misunderstands the quality of excrement that he overvalues what he wants to devalue – 'let dung and money be loved and valued alike'[10] – might be forgiven: he was an out and out townsman. But what about St Bernard, who said Cistercians 'see all that is most striking, most charming, as so much dung',[11] and the peasantry themselves, who knew from daily experience the virtue and value of excrement,[12] yet who made it the core of the language of abuse.

We know they valued it because it was kept where they could keep an eye on it, inside the house where the animals dropped it,[13] just outside the door,[14] in

[10] J.R.H. Moorman, *St. Francis of Assisi* (SPCK new ed. 1976), p. 36, cf *St. Francis of Assisi, his life and writings as recorded by contemporaries*, trans. and ed. Leo Sherley Price (1959), p. 28, and Lester K. Little, *Religious Poverty and the Profit Economy in Medieval Europe* (1978), p. 164.

[11] Quoted in Henry Kraus, *The Living Theatre of Medieval Art* (1967), p. 174.

[12] Whether it was Englishmen and their sheep, those 'four-footed muck spreaders, or rather, . . . mobile combinations of fertilizer manufacturers, distributors and spreaders, fetching their own raw materials and processing them, and delivering and applying their products' (Eric Kerridge, *The Farmers of Old England* (1973), p. 20), or north German farmers with theirs, continuously cultivating poor soils 'though an annual system of manuring known as *Plaggendüngung*' (Alan Mayhew, *Rural Settlement and Farming in Germany* (1973), p. 20), or north Chinese villagers and their pigs: 'Chairman Mao has said that each pig is a small fertilizer factory' (Jan Myrdal and Gun Kessle, *China: the Revolution Continued* (Penguin books 1973), p. 78).

[13] To the references cited in Dung A, note 7 might be added Eugen Weber, *Peasants into Frenchmen*, p. 149, where a traveller of the 1890s is quoted: 'A single compartment; men and beasts live fraternally, until the ones eat the others'; Flann O'Brien, *The Poor Mouth* (Pan Books 1975), pp. 18–20; Emmanuel le Roy Ladurie, *Montaillou* (Eng. trans 1975), pp. 40, 198.

[14] For instance in Lancashire, 'The Apostolical Life of Ambrose Barlow, O.S.B.,' ed. W.E. Rhodes, *The Downside*

the yard,[15] beside the front gate.[16] Moreover, in Sussex 'it was reckoned that the bailiff's boots were the best dung';[17] in other words a continually itinerant bailiff got the best out of an estate as manure got the best out of the land: no contempt there. Still, in Breton *Kaoc'h*, stronger than *merde*, combined with the words *ki* (dog) and *du* (black), is about the worst one can be called: shit of the devil!,[18] while in Ireland peasants forced to fight for James II at the Boyne apparently called him Seamus the Shit.[19] There is surely a connection of some kind here with our use, as words of hate, contempt and derision of the very words we use for copulation and for our genitalia, as well as those words we use of God, his son and his mother. We abuse most what we cherish most. Perhaps that is one line of enquiry.

Review, 44 (1926), p. 242. Compare the ox tethered at the door for all to see in seventeenth-century China, 'the treasured evidence of a family's status', Jonathan D. Spence, *The Death of Woman Wang* (1978), p. 72.

[15] For example, in Montaillou (Ladurie, *op. cit.*, p. 256), 'In the courtyard there was a big tall dungheap, from the top of which you could see through a chink in the wall what was going on in the *solier* |the first floor|, and in Pamiers (*ibid.*, pp. 146–7) where Arnaud de Verniolles, counterfeit priest, used them as 'beds' for his homosexual couplings with young lads. For urban pigs scavenging in urban dunghills see Edward A. Armstrong, *Saint Francis: Nature Mystic* (paperback ed. 1976) pp. 116–8. At Shugborough Hall in Staffordshire (now the County Museum) the midden yard survives with its 'fittings'. I would be pleased to learn of any other such survivals.

[16] 'Beside each gate was the family's privy hopefully placed at the edge of the public road in anticipation of a contribution to the domestic store of fertilizer from any traveller who might be in need of relief': William Hinton, *Fanshen* (Penguin Books 1972), p. 21. For Victorian 'dung'll holes', cesspool privies, 'pig tubs' and pigs see Edwin Grey, *Cottage Life in a Hertfordshire Village* (Harpenden 1977), pp. 50–1.

[17] Bob Copper, *A Song for Every Season* (1975), p. 10.

[18] *The horse of Pride*, p. 147.

[19] Thomas Flanagan, *The Year of the French* (paperback ed. 1980), p. 64.

Another might be the way in which the educated, urban elite has always regarded the peasant. Russian peasants were called stinkers (*smerdy*),[20] Dante wished 'the "stinking" peasants would leave Florence and go back to their wretched villages',[21] and Rutebeuf, the thirteenth-century French poet, said 'that when a villein died even Hell would not have him because he smelled too bad.'[22] The aversion the patrician townsman and aristocratic countryman felt for the dirty and dungy peasant farmer and labourer[23] transformed the language used to describe them: rustics, churls, boors, and villains are by *c.* 1200 no longer merely country dwellers of one sort or another but beasts, savages and degenerates, capable of every viciousness and moral depravity.[24] They are (by definition) not capable of any gentle or noble thought or action. In this fashion too might not dung as well as those who worked with it (to get not only their own living but that of those who called them names for their efforts) have got such a bad name? After all, like 'you peasant!', 'you shit!' is abusive.

In literature, as in life, that abusive connotation

[20] Jerome Blum, *Lord and Peasant in Russia* (paperback ed. 1971), p. 27.

[21] Alexander Murray, *Reason and Society in the Middle Ages* (1978), p. 239.

[22] Weber, *op. cit.*, p. 149.

[23] For instance, the Bishop of Silves in Portugal, Alvaro Poláez, *c.* 1320: even rich peasants 'work with their own hands . . . all day long they plough and dig the earth so that they are wholly *earthy*. They suck up earth, they eat it, they talk of earth, in their land they have placed all their hope', quoted in J.N. Hillgarth, *The Spanish Kingdoms 1250–1516*, I (1976), p. 120.

[24] Alexander Murray, *op. cit.*, pp. 237–39; J.H. Hexter, *The Vision of Politics on the Eve of the Reformation* (1973), pp. 194–98, esp. p. 197. And compare Weber, *op. cit.*, chapter one, 'A Country of Savages'.

could be readily evidenced, from Dafydd Ap Gwilym's vivid description of the jealous husband as a dunghill[25] to J.R.R. Tolkein's orcs who use coarse language: 'He knifed me, the dung'. There are, however, other associations, especially of nostalgic affection: Czeslaw Milosz, for instance, recalling his Lithuanian childhood 'squishing with my big toe the warm muck of the dunghill',[26] and Maigret waking up in the morning with a hangover:[27]

> 'A neuf heures et demie, il n'était pas encore levé. La fenêtre grande ouverte laissait depuis longtemps pénétrer les bruits du dehors, le caquet des poules qui grattaient le fumier dans une cour, la chaîne d'un chien, les appels insistants des remorqueurs et ceux, plus sourds, des péniches à moteur.'

Still, there is much more to it than that, as John Constable's picture of the Stour Valley and Dedham Village shows.[28] Constable, one of the finest and best of English countrymen, painted it in 1814 for a bridegroom to give his bride as a wedding present. It was not a surprise gift; it had been done with the approval of the bride's family who came from Constable's own East Bergholt. They saw nothing odd about the hill of muck in the foreground, a 'runover dungle' as it was called in Suffolk, originally 100

[25] 'Na cheisied, a'i fawed fo,
Hon Eiddig ei hun iddo'.
Her husband's death (I Eiddig), *Dafydd Ap Gwilym, Fifty Poems*, trans. and ed. H. Idris Bell and David Bell, Y Cymmrodor, XLVIII (1942), pp. 128–129.

[26] *Post-War Polish Poetry*, ed. and trans. Czeslaw Milosz (Penguin Books 1970), p. 63.

[27] *Maigret se fache* (Presses de la Cité 1957), p. 41.

[28] For what follows see Ian Fleming-Williams, 'A Runover Dungle and a Possible Date for Spring', *Burlington Magazine* 104 (1972), pp. 386–90.

feet long by six feet high, being dug out by two farm labourers.[29] No more should we. Just, therefore, as a dunghill was a suitable subject for a painting, dung was a proper one for a lecture. Much more than proper; essential, if an understanding of a vanished culture was to be engendered.

DUNG C

THEN, again, there is a fine story in Chuang Tzu which shows what the Taoists meant by 'the Way' or the 'Order of Nature'. His disciples were trying to find out what he meant by the Tao, and said: 'It surely can't be in those broken tiles over there?' He replied: 'Yes, it is in those broken tiles'. The disciples asked a series of such questions, and ended by saying: 'It surely can't be in that piece of dung?' But the reply was: 'Yes, it is everywhere'.[1]

In one corner of the yard was a pile of horse manure taller than an adult human being. 'Aiya! Aiya!' our parents, grandfathers, and neighbours exclaimed, eyes open in wonder as they stood around the pile, neighbours and friends invited especially to view it. 'Come here! Come look. Oh, just look at it!' – I could tell that the adults felt what I felt, that I did not feel it alone, but truly. This pile hummed, and it was the fuel for the ground, the toads, the vegetables, the house, the two grandfathers. The flies, which were green and turquoise-black and silvery blue, swirling into various lights, hummed too, like excess sparks. The grandfathers boxed the horse

[29] G.E. Evans, *The Horse in the Furrow* (1960), pp. 117–8, and for muck spreading, pp. 135–6.

[1] Joseph Needham, *The Grand Titration* (1969), p. 160.

manure, presents for us and their good friends to take home. They also bagged it in burlap. It smelled good.[2]

Even at that time, human dung was considered highly desirable as a fertilizer and presumably represented a good source of income. Later on, the removal of ordure in the big cities was concentrated in the hands of contractors who amassed great wealth from their business and whose children rose to the upper classes of society.[3]

In Grassano at almost regular hours, in the early morning and again in the evening, windows were surreptitiously opened and the wrinkled hands of old women were to be seen emptying the contents of chamber pots into the street. These were 'black magic' or bad luck hours. In Gagliano the ceremony was neither as widespread nor as regular; so precious a fertilizer for the fields could not be wasted.[4]

The practice on the downland farms of south Wiltshire at the end of the eighteenth century was to allow 1000 sheep to fold every night on one 'tenancy' acre, equal to two-thirds of the statutory acre. In other words, a south Wiltshire downland farm of the same size as the medieval virgate, i.e. one containing about 30 'tenancy' acres of arable, might require the dung of at least 100 sheep throughout the year. This ration was far and away in excess of what our south Wiltshire villages of the thirteenth century disposed of.[5]

Every day, within a radius of some thirty miles

[2] Maxine Hong Kingston, *China Men* (1981), p. 164.

[3] Werner Eichhorn, *Chinese Civilization: an Introduction* (1969), p. 267.

[4] Carlo Levi, *Christ Stopped at Eboli* (1947, Penguin Books 1982), p. 96.

[5] M.M. Postan, *Essays on Medieval Agriculture and General Problems of the Medieval Economy* (1973), p. 236.

from the city, large carts and wagons piled with hay
wended their way there, and returned on the following day loaded with manure that could be obtained
in London in plenty, almost for the asking. This
cheap and plentiful source of replenishment for the
Middlesex soil made it possible for a crop to be taken
away each season.[6]

Young strawberry sets were planted out in July or
August on south facing slopes of the Mendip Hills.
Bracken and heather were packed around each
plant to keep the berries out of the dirt and to
protect the crop from light frosts. Large quantities of
manure were needed to maintain the quality of the
soil and at the end of the nineteenth century a
Strawberry Growers Association was formed which
organised the bulk purchase of manure from the
cattle boats arriving at Bristol docks. The manure
was sent to Cheddar by train and allocated to the
growers according to the size of their strawberry
plots.[7]

Indeed, the prize-winning leek grower is something of an alchemist himself, feeding his beloved
vegetable during the long lonely hours at the allot-
ment with mysterious and secret concoctions of his
own making. Bill Williamson, who was born at
Throckley, tells us 'leeks have been fed on beer,
urine, blood and human waste. In one case a whole
family was barred from the lavatory for a fortnight
to provide a good supply of feeding material; in
another case, a Northumberland pitman fed his
leeks on the scrapings of the baby's nappy, and
swore blind that his leeks won because they'd been
fed on pure mother's milk'.[8]

[6] Walter Rose, *Good Neighbours* (1942), p. 78.
[7] Ann Heeley and Martyn Brown, *Victorian Somerset: Farming* (Friends of the Abbey Barn, Glastonbury, 1979), p. 45.
[8] John Gorman, *To Build Jerusalem* (1980), p. 105.

He tarried so long that he had to use the outhouse, but he carefully weighed his shit on the outhouse scales so that these neighbours could return a like amount to his fields.[9]

> So much emptiness
> is in itself a pleasure: in the crapper
> with my own specific ass.
> God state society family party . . .
> Out, the whole lot of you.
> What smells is me!
> If only I could weep.[10]

Is the development of the shit-house paradigmatic of the development of society: from the communal to the individual?[11]

Thomas Lovell challenges Sir Nicholas Bacon to a duel in 1586: 'But if thowe shalt refuse . . . then I will secretlye repute the, and openlye blase the, as a dunghell spyryted man'.[12]

A group of immigrants from Grassano used to meet every Sunday for an outing to the country after their hard week's work in New York . . . 'There were eight or ten of us: a doctor, a druggist, some trades-men, a hotel waiter, and a few workers, all of us from the same town and acquainted with each other since we were children. Life is depressing there among the skyscrapers, where there's every possible convenience, elevators, revolving doors, subways, endless streets and buildings, but never a bit of green earth. Home-sickness used to get the better of us. On Sundays we took a train for miles and miles in search of some open country. When finally we

[9] Maxine Hong Kingston, *China Men* (1981), p. 22.
[10] Günter Grass, *The Flounder* (1978), p. 240.
[11] A thought: in the British Museum north staircase lavatory 25 May 1984.
[12] A. Hassell Smith, *County and Court: Government and Politics in Norfolk 1558–1603* (1974), p. 184.

reached a deserted spot, we were all as happy as if a great weight had been lifted from our shoulders. And beneath a tree, all of us together would let down our trousers . . . What joy! We could feel the fresh air and all of nature around us. It wasn't like those American toilets, shiny and all alike. We felt like boys again, as if we were back in Grassano; we were happy, we laughed and we breathed for a moment the air of home. And when we had finished we shouted together: *"Viva l'Italia!"* The words came straight from our hearts'.[13]

The long latrines lay beyond the men's camp, and arriving there the boy stepped over the plank on which men sat while defecating. An arm either side of the pit, he lowered himself, trying to find knee and toe-holds in either wall. The stench blinded him and flies invaded his mouth and ears and nostrils. As he entered the larger foulness and touched the bottom of the pit, he seemed to hear what he believed to be a hallucinatory murmur of voices behind the rage of flies. Were they behind you? said one voice. And another said, Dammit, this is our place!

There were ten children in there with him.[14]

Time and again I asked the Germans the question which in those days was on everyone's mind. 'How could such terrible things happen in one of the world's most cultured countries?' And time and again the answer would come back 'Was uns gefehlt hat war die Gabe der Unterscheidung der Geister' – 'What we lacked was the gift for the discernment of spirits'. Naturally I understood what, in the literal sense, they meant by this phrase: they meant that

[13] Carlo Levi, *Christ Stopped at Eboli* (1947, Penguin Books 1982), pp. 96–7.
[14] Thomas Keneally, *Schindler's Ark* (1982, Coronet Books 1983), pp. 259–60.

they had underestimated the power of evil that had been awakened in Germany by the rise of the National Socialists. But for more than a quarter of a century the phrase haunted me, and as I turned it over in my mind, I always suspected that there was more to it than the literal sense. Yet the profounder meaning of it only began to emerge for me a quarter of a century later with an incident in the locker room of the Sports Centre of the Santa Cruz campus. There one day I heard an instructor talking to a student about *Justine* (which I later discovered was a novel by the Marquis de Sade). He was saying that from the novel one could learn that 'once you can eat shit, then you can do anything'. The instructor, I might say, was commending this process as one of liberation, as if to say, once you have broken through the barrier that divides shit from food then there are no limits to what you can do.

But for me the remark took on a darker meaning and it instantly, if obscurely, associated itself in my mind with a lack of the spirit of discretion, or *discretio spiritum*, as the Vulgate translates that phrase of St Paul in the letter to the Corinthians. Searching for the roots of that obscure association I turned towards the roots of the word *discretio* and discovered, to my astonishment, that it is derived from the Greek word which means 'shit'; so that the person who lacks discretion in the deepest sense of the word, is one who does not recognise shit for what it is; who, in the words of the regimental song of the RAOC, 'can't tell sugar from shit'; who is so devoid of discretion that he will eat it as if it were sugar.[15]

I will sweep away the house of Jeroboam as a man sweeps dung away till none is left, says Yahweh.[16]

[15] Donald Nicholl, 'The Catholic Church and the Nazis', *Christian*, vol. 5, no. 1 (All Souls, 1978), p. 10.
[16] I Kings 14, v. 10.

Goldwell House, Aldington: the attics, with remains of cow-dung partition, dividing the sleeping quarters of the male servants from those of the female. The Holy Maid slept here until November 1525.[17]

'Then he sayde that if he hade the Roode that standeth in the monasterye of Eye he wolde brenne it. And he wolde shyte upon the hed to make it a foot hygher than it is nowe.'[18]

'He should honour God as well with a forkfull of muck as with a wax candle.'[19]

St Ignatius Loyola: 'I am mere dung . . .'[20]

Addle Street . . . may well have had the special meaning 'lane full of cow-dung' or the like. OE *adela* seems to have been used especially of stinking urine. OSwed *ko-adel* means 'cow urine' and MLG *adel*, *eddel* 'liquid manure'. This is, of course, a doubtful case.[21]

Gong (Anglo-Saxon and Old English) is a privy: 'I knoweleche to the that ther hys no goonge more stynkynge thenne my soule is' (*The Lay Folks Mass Book*). Gong farmer is the dung agent who cleared the cesspit, usually at night: 'No goungfermour shall carry any ordure till after nine of the clocke in the night' (Stow's *Survey of London*).[22]

---

[17] Alan Neame, *The Holy Maid of Kent: the Life of Elizabeth Barton 1506–1534* (1971), illustration.

[18] George Glazener, shoemaker of Eye, 1532: Margaret Cook, 'Eye, Suffolk, in the Years of Uncertainty 1520–1590' (unpublished Keele University Ph.D. thesis, 1981), p. 102.

[19] John Norgate of Aylesham, Norfolk, 1537: John F. Davis, *Heresy and Reformation in the South East of England 1520–1559* (1983), p. 86.

[20] Jean Delumeau, *Catholicism between Luther and Voltaire* (English translation, 1977), p. 43.

[21] E. Ekwall, *Street Names of the City of London* (1954), p. 55.

[22] *The Oxford New English Dictionary*, sub Gong.

Foldyard and midden at Blencarn, Cumberland.[23]

Savonarola was to preach on Ascension Day, May 4 1497, and the previous night some young men managed to enter the Duomo and fill the pulpit with filth.[24]

A group of youths at Christmas 1498 took a wagon of manure and walled up the residence of the Milanese ambassador.[25]

There was in those days, and had been for years, a vexed question between Hopkins and Jolliffe the bailiff on the matter of – stable manure. Hopkins had pretended to the right of taking what he required from the farmyard, without asking leave of anyone. Jolliffe in return had hinted that if this were so, Hopkins would take it all. 'But I can't eat it,' Hopkins had said. Jolliffe merely grunted, signifying by the grunt, as Hopkins thought, that though a gardener couldn't eat a mountain of manure fifty feet long and fifteen high – couldn't eat in the body – he might convert it into things edible for his own personal use. And so there had been a great feud.[26]

Red Cloud told his agent, 'Father, the Great Spirit did not make us to work, He made us to hunt and fish. He gave us the plains and the hills and covered them with the buffalo. He filled the streams and rivers with the fish. The white man can work if he wants to, but the Great Spirit did not make *us* to work. The white man owes us a living for the lands he has taken.' Sitting Bull was more brief: 'I don't want anything to do with a people who make an

[23] Olive Cook, *English Cottages and Farmhouses* (1982), illustration 40 cf *Dung B* note 15.

[24] M. Creighton, *A History of the Papacy* (1903), vol. iv, p. 264. I owe this reference to my friend Dr John Law.

[25] R. Trexler, 'Florentine Theatre, 1280–1500', *Forum Italicum*, vol. 14, number 3 (1980). And this one too.

[26] Anthony Trollope, *The Small House at Allington* (Oxford Classics 1981), p. 655.

Indian warrior to carry water on his shoulders or haul manure.'[27]

E. Delcambre has collected a particularly important documentation on Lorraine at the end of the sixteenth and during the seventeenth centuries. With him we may recall (amongst other facts) the offerings at St Benedict's Church in Brecklange. A peasant from Saint-Dié had dislocated his hip, and his neighbour promised to mend it by begging manure from nine different stables, filling the peasant's breeches which he had been wearing at the time of the accident with it and hanging them up in the church. In the same sanctuary a woman healer (*guérriseuse*) brought in pilgrimage, for the cure of a sick person, a man's stocking containing five eggs and three handfuls of horse-dung put there by the patient's daughter. A rite like this is explained on the hypothesis that the sickness was like a poison, represented here by excrement. The saint would destroy the sickness via the offering.[28]

A man named Yann K never failed to walk across one or another of his fields at dawn, before the sun had completely risen. After a short while, he would suddenly feel like 'undoing his breeches' or 'squatting down'. With the sharp edge of his spade, he'd cut a cube of earth out of the side of a slope facing away from the road. Then, with great care, he would proceed to relieve himself into the hole. When he had finished, he would consider what had come out of him. The consistency was good and the colour was fine. Our man would put the cube of earth back with his spade and make his way home, whistling and light of foot. All was well: there was nothing to

[27] Rex Alan Smith, *Moon of Popping Trees* (1975, Bison Books 1981), p. 60.
[28] Jean Delumeau, *Catholicism between Luther and Voltaire* (English Translation 1977), pp. 162–3.

worry about. He would not think of death for the whole day.[29]

When you go outside to ease yourself, take your mattock, dig a hole and cover your excrement.[30]

You know, sir, she's a fine lady, my sister is. She plays the piano, she talks Spanish. And, you'd never believe it of the sister of the humble employee who's taking you up in the lift, but she denies herself nothing; Madame has a maid to herself, and she'll have her own carriage one day, I shouldn't wonder. She's very pretty, if you could see her, a bit too high and mighty, but well, you can understand that. She's full of fun. She never leaves a hotel without relieving herself first in a wardrobe or a drawer, just to leave a little keepsake with the chambermaid who'll have to clean up. Sometimes she does it in a cab, and after she's paid her fare, she'll hide behind a tree, and she doesn't half laugh when the cabby finds he's got to clean his cab after her ... But I'm keeping you babbling' (I had not uttered a single word and was beginning to fall asleep as I listened to the flow of his). 'Good-night, sir. Oh! thank you, sir. If everybody had as kind a heart as you, there wouldn't be any poor people left. But, as my sister says, "there must always be poor people so that now that I'm rich I can shit on them". You'll pardon the expression. Good-night, sir.'[31]

He raises the poor from the dust
He lifts the needy from the dunghill
To give them a place with princes
And to assign them a seat of honour[32]

[29] Pierre-Jakez Hélias, *The Horse of Pride* (English translation 1978), p. 266.
[30] Deuteronomy 23, vs. 12–14.
[31] Marcel Proust, *Remembrance of Things Past* (1981), volume two, p. 1012.
[32] Hannah's Song: I Samuel 2.

His greatest ambition was to produce a work consisting entirely of quotations.[33]

[33] Hannah Arendt on Walter Benjamin in the introduction to his *Illuminations* (English translation 1970), p. 4.

13

Can a Novelist be a Saint?

A SAINT, whatever else he may be, has to be good at his job. An incompetent postman or an inefficient window-cleaner can no more be a saint than an unfatherly father or an unkingly king. Thus, a saintly novelist must be a good one. Even a great one, as St Catherine of Genoa was a great hospital administrator and St Thomas More a great humanist. On this score there are a number of contenders. Henry James, for example, for whom it was better to be deceived than to be a deceiver, or Marcel Proust, who died that his novel might live, or Malcolm Lowry, who was no less a martyr to his art. There is, there has to be of course, much more to it than that. Let us take a case.

Janko M. was born near Bardejov in Slovakia in 1902. The son of a peasant farmer, he grew up in the village his father's family had lived in since the seventeenth century. He came to manhood amid sheep, barley and flax, smelling the scents of mown hay and farmyard dung. In summer there were cherries, in autumn, hazelnuts. The flowers at Corpus Christi were from the woodland beyond the river Topla. At Christmas he struggled with the other altar boys for the marzipan stars thrown into the snow by the priest; one Easter he went with his parents and brothers and sisters on pilgrimage to Levoča. He tended sheep with his uncles and cousins; once he travelled with some of them into what was still Russia and saw the ghetto in Grybów. In 1912 in Bardejov he saw a motor car and a moving picture show. He caught trout with his fingers, could handle the farmhorses better than his father or brothers, and played the 'fujara' as well as anyone could remember it being played. The first world war passed his village by: the guns rumbled the other side of the mountains. By then he had been reading with an ease which the new village priest, unlike his predecessor, took sharp notice of. Janko was sent to the school in Bardejov. There he learnt to write and, when the government of the new Czechoslovakia expanded its staff in the town, he went to work in the sixteenth-century townhall as a clerk. That was in 1919.

He was good at his job; throughout the 1920s he was steadily promoted. He visited his parents often, helped with the harvest, attended his brothers' weddings, and with them and the women one night in 1927 sat wake beside his father's body in the parlour whose walls were decorated with faded lithographs of the Virgin and the Man of Sorrows. He had a few short stories published in the literary journals of Bratislava; they were about the passions and *longeurs* of Slovakian small town life, in a style unadorned and atmospheric; rightly, they were praised. In 1932 what turned out to be his only novel, *An Easter Incident*, was published in Prague. It was acclaimed in the capital but, owing to the Slovakian in which it was written, its 'highbrow' nature, and its subject matter, it neither reached a large audience nor made any money for its author.

An Easter Incident relates in a· sparse but never other than limpid style the story of František Kollar, a devout village baker, who one Good Friday, when the religious enthusiasm of his fellow villagers becomes unrestrained and violence is offered to the single Jewish family in the community, gives them sanctuary and calms the hysteria of priest and people. František does this not so much by eloquence as by a hitherto unnoticed (because uncalled forth) presence or, as we might say nowadays, 'charisma'. Janko M. may have based his novel on an actual event. In Mukachevo in 1930 an Easter procession had by ill fortune encountered a group of pious Jewish youths returning from the ritual bath; stones had been thrown when hats had not been removed; fighting had followed, but had ceased as quickly as it had begun; there had only been cuts and bruises. There was more drama in the novel than in the Ruthenian affair; nonetheless, the fictional incident was underplayed too. Yet it was timeless. Janko's greatness as a novelist consists in his suggestion of that quality, indeed, in his utterly convincing the reader of it. After his saving action, František Kollar is ostracised by his fellow Christians; they continue to buy his bread – he is not the village's only baker, his bread is simply the best – but he becomes a pariah, an outcast within the community. His Christian devotion is undiminished; solitary at the front of the church, set apart by his neighbours who cluster at the rear, he is denied confession and communion by a bigoted priest. František falters, is full of doubts, tends to despondency: this is delicately rendered by Janko, no more than sketched in yet with a firmness which leaves the reader tense with compassion. The novel ends with the slightest of miracles; a door opens, light briefly streams in where no light should be: we are aware that František knows his Good

Friday action has been right. No synopsis can do this sensitive and perfectly observed novel justice. It is a tragedy it has not been translated.

After its publication Janko M. continued to live as he had lived previously: he worked in the government office in Bardejov, from time to time wrote short stories which were published, and spent almost all his free time on his family's farm, where each summer until 1941 he turned the hay and handled the horses hitched to the harvest wagon. There was one change. By 1934 he had become head of his department. In September 1938 he was promoted to head of department at Prešov. It was from his office there, in a battlemented house of the seventeenth century where beneath his window under the rowan trees which lined the street countrywomen sat selling cucumbers and green peaches, that Janko observed the destruction of Czechoslovakia and the creation of the German puppet state of Slovakia. It was from there too that he obstructed as effectively as his position allowed (and even beyond) the registration of Jewish property, the marking with the star of David of letters sent by Jews, the confiscation of Jewish valuables by the Hlinka Guard, and, when they began in March 1942, the deportation to Germany of Slovakian Jews. He was particularly successful in protecting Jewish 'converts' to christianity, in obtaining for Jews 'protective letters' certifying that the bearers were essential to the economy, and from 1943 in helping Jews to escape to Hungary. After the Slovak rising of August 1944 and the intervention of *Einsatzgruppe H.* under *Obersturmbannführer* Vitezka, which rounded up almost all the remaining Jews in Slovakia, he could do no more except join those whom hitherto he had helped. Under false papers long before prepared and long held in readiness, the star of David sewn at last upon his jacket, Janko M. mingled with those being herded together under the rowan trees. He perished at Auschwitz in October 1944.

Such is the case; it is entirely hypothetical. By way of justifying the novelist as saint it requires little further comment. There have been other, similar heroes, many more than the few who are celebrated: Oskar Schindler, Otto Schimek, Anton Schmidt, Franz Jägerstätter. One has been canonised: Maximillian Kolbe. Still, saving one's fellow men or refusing to destroy one's fellow Christians is one thing, heroic as it is; going against the grain of one's own culture, as Ariadna Skryabina and Fräulein Lange went against the grain of their urban, cultivated worlds to become Jews and so to die with their new brothers and sisters, is surely another. Moreover, Janko M.'s was a Christian, peasant culture. He did not desert it: every Christmas and Easter he went with his family to the village church just as he went with them to the fields in summer. Twice in the 1930s he went on pilgrimage, once again to Levoča and for the first time to Staré Hory. His rosary survives. It was also an East European Christian peasant culture; centuries of hostility to Jews were embedded in it. How did Janko transcend that antagonism, first in his novel, then, in imitation of his own great art, in his life, and finally in his sacrifice? What gifts of spiritual power was he given, did he cultivate? Was the writing of the novel, such a gem of artistic and intellectual integrity, preparation for the life and ultimately the death which succeeded it? And how had life, his peasant Christian life, fitted him for the writing of the novel? Probably, undoubtedly, none of these questions matters. What does is that Janko M., Christian, peasant, and novelist, would be a *zaddik* to Jews. And ought to be to Christians.